THE KNIFE THAT KILLED ME

ALSO BY ANTHONY MCGOWAN

Hellbent

Jack Tumor
Winner of the UK's Booktrust
Teenage Prize and Catalyst Award

THE KNIFE THAT KILLED ME

anthony mcgowan

DELACORTE PRESS

Copyright © 2008 by Anthony McGowan

All rights reserved. Published in the United States by Delacorte Press, an imprint of
Random House Children's Books, a division of
Random House, Inc., New York.
Originally published in paperback in Great Britain by Definitions,
an imprint of Random House Children's Books, a division of the Random House Group,
Ltd., London, in 2008.

Delacorte Press is a registered trademark and the colophon is a trademark
of Random House, Inc.

Visit us on the Web! www.randomhouse.com/teens

Educators and librarians, for a variety of teaching tools, visit us at
www.randomhouse.com/teachers

Library of Congress Cataloging-in-Publication Data
McGowan, Anthony.
The knife that killed me / Anthony McGowan.—1st. American ed.
p. cm.
Summary: Paul Varderman, a secondary student in an English Catholic School, is a loner
until, just as he is becoming friends with "the freaks," the school bully encourages Paul to
join his gang and gives him a knife to carry as an incentive.
ISBN 978-0-385-73822-4 (hc)—ISBN 978-0-385-90716-3 (lib. bdg.)—
ISBN 978-0-375-89392-6 (e-book)
[1. Gangs—Fiction. 2. Bullies—Fiction. 3. Catholic schools—Fiction. 4. Schools—
Fiction. 5. Friendship—Fiction. 6. Murder—Fiction. 7. England—Fiction.] I. Title.
PZ7.M16912Kni 2010
[Fic]—dc22
2009011662

The text of this book is set in 12-point Goudy.

Book design by Kenny Holcomb

Printed in the United States of America

10 9 8 7 6 5 4 3 2 1

First American Edition

TO LIAM ANTHONY MCGOWAN
(1968–2007)

ONE

The knife that killed me was a special knife. Its blade was inscribed with magical runes from a lost language, and the metal glimmered with a thousand colors, iridescent as a peacock's tail or the slick of petrol on a puddle. It was made from a meteorite that had plunged to Earth after a journey of a hundred million miles. The heat of entry burned off its crust of brittle rock, leaving a core of iron infused with traces of iridium, titanium, platinum and gold. It was first forged into a blade in ancient Persia, where, set in a hilt of ivory and rhino horn, it passed from hand to hand, worshipped and feared for its power. From Persia it was looted by Alexander the Great, who plucked it from the fingers of King Darius as he lay dying. With Alexander it went to India, where it severed the tendons of the war elephants of Porus, leaving the beasts to vent their fury on the dry earth with thrashing tusks. With Alexander's death the blade was lost to history for three hundred years before it emerged again, taken by Julius Caesar from the royal treasury of Cleopatra. For two centuries it was worn by Roman emperors, and this was the knife that the mad Caligula used to cut the child from his sister's womb. The blade went east again with Valerian, to subdue the barbarians. Five legions perished in the desert, pierced by Parthian arrows, and the emperor's last sight on this earth was his own knife as it cut out his eyes. And for how long did he feel the cool intensity of its edge as he was flayed, and his skin made into a fleshy bag for horseshit, a gory trophy for the victor's temple? From Parthians it passed to Arabs, driven in their conquest by the fervor of faith. And then, at parley, the brave but covetous eye of Richard *Coeur de Lion* saw the glimmer in Saladin's belt, and that noble Saracen gave up the knife for the sake of peace. With Richard it arrived at last in England. Again a thing of secret worship, dark rites, unholy acts, it moved like an illness of the blood from generation to generation, exquisite but cursed. Until finally, after its journey of eons, it came to me and found its home in my heart.

Yes, a special knife; a cruel knife; a subtle knife.

I wish.

Well, I've had a long time to think about it.

So, now, the truth.

The knife that killed me wasn't a special knife at all. It didn't have any runes on it. Its handle wasn't made of ivory and rhino horn, but cheap black plastic. It was a kitchen knife from Woolworths, and its blade wobbled like a loose tooth.

But it did the job.

TWO

I'm in a gray place now. It could be worse, as hells go. I always thought that hell would burn you, but here I'm cold.

They've told me to write it all out. Why it happened. Why I did it. They said I had to write the truth. But then they said I had to use nice words, so half of this is a lie, because the real words weren't nice at all. You'll have to imagine those words, the ones that aren't nice. I'm sure you can manage that.

No computers here. Just paper and a pen and a big old dictionary, so I get the spelling right.

So I'm remembering. And you know how it is when you remember things. They get jumbled up, the old with the new, the now with the then. But sometimes I find the place and I'm there, utterly, completely, and the people are talking and moving and I'm with them again.

Like now.

I am in a field. The gypsy field, next to the school. There are bodies around me. Bodies entwined. Arms move up and down. Bodies fall. Feet stamp.

When it began, there were shouts, screams, sounds that seemed to come out of the middle of guts and chests, not out of mouths at all. But now there are only the low grunts of hard effort and lower moans from the fallen. And I am among them, but not one of them—one of the fighters, I mean.

I have seen a face I know. Eyes wide with terror. A bigger face is above the face I know, animal hands holding it, the knuckles on the fingers white with the work of it. And the big face has bared its teeth, and the teeth move to the smaller face, the face I know, and the teeth rake down the face, frustrated, not getting purchase, slipping over the tight skin, the shaven head.

I did not know that it would come to this, to biting, to eating.

Are we truly beasts?

I am pushed to the ground, my knees leaving hollows in the wet earth. And I want to move. Either away or toward. To do something. But I have been burned to this spot, like one of the ashy bodies cooked to stillness in Pompeii. Only my eyes can move.

But that's enough for me to see it coming.

The knife that will kill me.

It is in the hand of a boy.

The boy is blurred, but the knife is clear.

He has just taken it from the inside pocket of his blazer.

There is something strange about the way the world is moving. I can see an outline of his arm—I mean, a series of outlines—tracing the motion from his pocket. A ghost trail of outlines. And so there is no motion, just these images, each one still, each one closer to me.

He is coming to kill me.

Now would be a good time to run.

I cannot run.

I am too afraid to run.

But I don't want to die here in the gypsy field, my blood flowing into the wet earth.

I must stop this.

And there is a way.

It comes to me now.

Part of it but not all of it.

Maths. Mr. McHale. A sunny afternoon, and no one listening. He tells us about Zeno's Paradox. The one with fast-running Apollo and the tortoise. If only I could remember it. But I'm not good at school. All I know about is war, battles, armies, learned from my dad, whose chief love is war.

But I have to remember, because the knife is coming. Each moment perfectly still, yet each one closer.

Motion

and

perfect

stillness.

How can that be?

Yes, I think. To reach me the knife must come half the way. That takes, say, two seconds. But first it must go half that distance. Which takes one second. And half *that* distance, which takes half a second. And half that distance, which takes a quarter of a second. And so it goes on. Each time halving the distance and halving the time: $2+1+\frac{1}{2}+\frac{1}{4}+\frac{1}{8}+\frac{1}{16}$. The sequence is infinite. It means he can never reach me. I am safe.

And so I can leave the *me* there, the *me* now, waiting forever for the knife, while I go back to the beginning.

THREE

I was sitting in front of Roth and two of his mates. Not really right to call them mates. Roth didn't have mates. He had kids who did what he said. They were sniggering and whispering and I knew something bad was going to happen. I just didn't realize it was going to be happening to me.

It was geography, and Mr. Boyle was talking. He had a beard and wonky plastic glasses. Quite often he'd try to straighten them, but they just went from being wonky on one side to wonky on the other. The wonky glasses made him look mad, but he wasn't mad, just boring. He was wearing a

brown jacket that looked like it was made out of the dead re-
mains of many other jackets, and his trousers were too short
and showed that the left sock was red and the right sock
was blue.

Mr. Boyle had been at the school for a long time and
he didn't bother anyone.

I was looking out of the window. On that side of the
school you could see houses going on forever. You couldn't
see *my* house, but it was out there somewhere, in that red sea
of brick. I imagined floating out over the roofs, looking down
on the world below. I couldn't touch it, and it couldn't touch
me. Perfect.

Then I felt something hit the back of my head. It didn't
hurt. It wasn't like they were throwing rocks. Just a little tap.
I thought it was probably rolled-up paper, most likely mixed
with a gob of spit.

I felt a spasm of anger and embarrassment in my stomach. Once they started they didn't stop until they'd finished
with you. My hair was quite long—long all over. More because I didn't like having it cut than for any other reason.
When you have your hair cut, a person is looking at you and
just you, and I don't like that.

And I didn't like having stuff thrown at my hair. But
still, I had no choice but to ignore it. If you're in a gang, you
don't have to ignore things like people throwing balls of wet
paper at you. But when you're on your own, you do. You put
up with that, and much worse than that. In fact, if Roth's in-
volved, then even being in a gang won't help you much.

I felt more hits. And heard more sniggering. I could feel that I was blushing. That might seem weird to you, but one of the main things about getting picked on is it makes you ashamed. I felt a pressure building up inside me, made out of the shame mixed up with anger and fear. Some of the other kids in the class noticed what was happening. Some of them looked at me and then looked away, feeling bad, feeling pity. Some joined in with the sniggering, glad it wasn't them.

Mr. Boyle was still talking, still fiddling with his crooked glasses. He was saying, ". . . and the Great Lakes of North America—that's Lake Huron, Lake Michigan, Lake Ontario, Lake Erie and Lake Superior—contain more fresh water than all the, *ah*, other lakes, all of them, in the world . . . ," and his eyes seemed so far away they were actually looking at the Great Lakes. He certainly wasn't seeing what was happening right here in front of him.

I put my hand to the back of my head. I knew instantly that something was wrong, wronger even than I thought. There were lumps. Stuck in my hair. Sticky lumps. Paper-and-spit balls wouldn't have stayed in my hair like that. And the tackiness went onto my fingers, but the stuff wouldn't come out of my hair. I smelled my fingers. There was a sickly smell, half sour spit, half mint, and I realized it was chewing gum. They'd thrown little bits of chewing gum in my hair.

I turned round.

Roth in the middle. On one side there was a kid called Miller and on the other a kid called Bates. Roth's face was completely blank. You had to be frightened of Roth. It was almost funny how much he looked like a Stone Age man— I mean, like a cartoon of one. You half expected to see him wearing animal furs and carrying a big wooden club, maybe dragging a mammoth behind him. His jaw stuck out and his head sloped back and his arms seemed to reach right down to the ground.

He looked thick, but he wasn't thick. He knew where you were weak, and would use it to hurt you.

Like my hair.

He only had two expressions. There was his wolfish, laughing face, which he used when he was hitting someone, or there was his completely blank look, unblinking, emotionless.

That was the look you got when he was about to hit you.

He was blank now, and his black eyes stared straight into mine. It was like being stabbed.

But it wasn't Roth who'd been throwing bits of stinking chewing gum into my hair.

Nor was it Miller. I felt a bit sorry for Miller. There weren't many black kids at our school, because black kids are usually Protestant, and this was a Catholic school, and his way of fitting in was to suck up to the hardest kid in the year. I'd probably have done the same, if I'd had a choice. I don't think he had any natural evil in him, but there was nothing he wouldn't do if Roth gave him the nod. Miller was smiling, a sort of cringing smile, nodding his head up and down, and when I looked at him, he looked away out of the window for a second, and then at Roth, and then out of the window again, still smiling.

It was Bates who was doing most of the sniggering. Bates really *was* thick. His fringe went straight across his forehead, which made him look sort of mental. When he smiled, thick lines of spittle crisscrossed his lips. His nails were bitten down to ragged stumps, oozing blood. It made you wince to look at his nails, almost as if you could feel him gnawing and biting at them. He still had a piece of rolled-up chewing gum in his fingers.

The anger burned and bubbled inside me like lava in a volcano. My jaws were clamped together, and I could feel my lips tight across my teeth. Bates stopped sniggering. He tried to do a version of the hard Roth stare. But he couldn't stop his lips from curling into that spit-thick grin. I wanted to hit him. Really wanted to hit him. And I hated him enough, in that moment, not to care what happened to me afterward. Getting my head kicked in mattered to me less, just then, than having chewing gum in my hair.

But there was something else, something stronger than the rage. The embarrassment. I was still embarrassed—worse, humiliated—about being the one who was picked out. I knew the whole class was aware of this. Aware of the fact that I was the weak one they'd found. It turned my muscles to jelly. I had nothing to hit him with.

"Will you give over."

That was it. That was all I said.

Bates looked at me in mock seriousness for a second, as if I'd made a reasonable suggestion that he was considering.

"Paul Varderman, will you turn round, please."

It was Mr. Boyle, who'd finally noticed something. The back of my head.

I turned round, thinking that now it would stop. That was stupid. Less than a minute passed, and then another piece of stinking gum landed in my hair.

That did it. The shame and rage all came together in a hot rush to my face. I stood up quickly, so quickly that the chair fell back with a clatter to the floor. Now everyone was watching, not just me thinking they were. Mr. Boyle's mouth was open, stopped somewhere in the middle of the Great Lakes.

I spun round to face Bates again.

"Filthy dog," I spat out. I wanted to hit him, but I was still weak, still burning with the humiliation.

"Varderman, sit . . ."

The class were laughing now, enjoying it. This was great. Some drama, some spectacle. Much better than the Great Lakes and all that boring water. Bates laughed like an ape. Miller laughed. Even Roth seemed to smile.

". . . down, I said sit . . ."

I couldn't stand having the eyes of the class on me, their laughter in my ears.

". . . down."

But Mr. Boyle had lost control. The laughter of the class became insane, mixed with mad shouts. Other kids had stood up. Other chairs were thrown across the floor. Mr. Boyle looked around frantically, not knowing what to do. And then his eyes came back to me, the cause of it all. And he came wading toward me, barging aside kids and desks.

"Right, have it your way," he was shouting. "Get straight to—"

And the next thing I knew I was flying, looking down on the scene. It took me a moment to realize what was happening. Mr. Boyle was shouting in my ear. He'd picked me up. He was stronger than he looked. I don't know what he was shouting—it was just noise. And then, instead of carrying me, he was dragging me. And jumbled up with the meaningless noise I heard the dreaded words "Mr. Mordred's office." Mr. Boyle threw me out into the corridor, and I staggered a few steps. I looked back. Mr. Boyle's face was red. He wasn't wearing his glasses. They must have fallen off. He looked naked without them.

"Wait outside Mr. Mordred's office," he yelled at me. "And you tell him exactly why I sent you."

Is he closer? I can see his face now. It is not a good face. The white skin is pasted straight onto the bones, with no flesh to soften the line. The face looks like it was baked hard in a furnace. Tight, hard, inhuman. Except for the gash, the red and pink wound, caused by the mouth of another boy. And who is to say what I would do if my face had been chewed like that, torn open by the teeth of my enemies? But I must concentrate, must prove that Zeno is right, that Apollo can never catch the tortoise. Stay there, knife boy, stay there.

FOUR

I didn't go straight to Mordred's office. First I went to the toilets. I couldn't see the balls of chewing gum, but I felt for them with my fingers, and tried to tease them out. *Filthy dog. I said filthy dog. It was so stupid. I should have said something better.* The foul stuff had become so tangled up in my hair that pulling at it just seemed to make things worse. *Why did I say filthy dog?* So I went to the art block, found an empty room and took some scissors from a desk. *Something better. I should have said something funny, something that made him feel small.* Then I went back to the toilets and hacked at the hair wherever it was smeared with the gum. It took ten minutes, and at the end the sink was full of knotted clumps of hair. *Or hit him. Right in the face. Made him eat his teeth.* Then I washed my hands in water as hot as I could stand it, rubbing in the grimy soap, trying to get the rank stench of spit and mint off my fingers. *Filthy dog.* I didn't have time to take the scissors back to the art room, so I slipped them in my pocket. *But it was me who looked stupid. Godgodgodgodgodgod.*

I thought about going home. But if I went home after being sent to Mordred's office, I'd be in bad trouble. That was a definite suspension. Almost funny. You play truant and they punish you by kicking you out of school. But that wouldn't be the real punishment. The real punishment would be what my dad would do to me.

But it might all still be OK. What I'd done wasn't that bad. I couldn't tell Mordred or Boyle about Bates and the chewing gum, because that would be squealing, but even so, all I'd done was stand up in class and shout, "Filthy dog." I wish I hadn't said *filthy dog.* I wish I'd said something better or nothing at all.

So I went to Mordred's office, running back through the empty corridors. I could see into the classrooms through the little square windows. There were threads of wire running through the middle of the glass so you couldn't smash it. Some of the classrooms were full of the brainy kids, the ones who did their work, and I liked the look of the orderly rows and the way the kids listened and the way the teachers taught them things and didn't just try to stop them from fighting.

When I started school, I just got put into a class with the thick kids, and so I was one. Or at least no one ever told me I wasn't. I think things would have been different if they'd just said, *Here, go in this class*, and it was a good class. Because I wanted to learn things, not just about war. But once you're in a place you just can't get to another place.

And then I reached the part of the school with the staff room and the offices. It goes like this. You turn right at the end of the corridor, then the staff room is on your left, and the general office is opposite, on the right. Ahead there are some double doors. You go through there and you get to Mr. Mordred's room and, beyond that, the headmaster's office.

I didn't know anyone who'd ever been in the headmaster's office. The headmaster was called Mr. O'Tool. We don't often see Mr. O'Tool. Sometimes he walks around the school, taking a sort of black cloud of doom with him. He usually says something at the weekly assembly, but even when he's reading out the sports results and we've won at rounders or football, he'll sound like he's reading the casualty lists from the Battle of the Somme. Everyone thought that Mr. Mordred was after his job, and Mr. O'Tool looked like he thought there was nothing he could do about it.

There were two comfy chairs outside Mr. O'Tool's office, but only a row of hard chairs outside Mordred's door. Two boys and a girl were already sitting there. The girl looked like she'd been crying, and there were leaves and bits of twig in the back of her hair. I didn't know her name, but I'd seen her around. I thought she might have been caught, you know, in the bushes. But not with either of the ones sitting here. They were little Year Eight scruffs, spiky-haired, cheeky, but frightened. They'd probably gone too far in some prank, and now they were staring vacantly into space, the way you do when you're waiting to be punished.

I felt a bit calmer now I'd got that filth out of my hair, and the rage and the disgust and the humiliation of the whole thing had eased up, the way a toothache sometimes goes away after a while. But, as I waited, other feelings floated to the surface. The unfairness of everything, of me being here, while Roth and his lot got away with it. And the fear of what Mordred was going to do. And what if I did get permanently expelled? Dad would kill me for definite. Except you can only die once, and that pleasure would wait for me at Temple Moor High School. Because the only place that would take you if you got expelled from our school was Temple Moor, and Temple Moor kids hated us because of the war that had been going on for years. And any of our kids who washed up at the Temple would get massacred. Every day.

The bell went for the end of the lesson. It meant break was beginning, which meant that Mordred would be here to tear our heads off.

I heard a clomping sound coming down the corridor. For a second I thought it was Mordred, but then I remembered that Mordred had little feet and took little steps and made a tippy-tap sound when he walked. I looked up and saw Mr. Boyle. His glasses were even more skewed than usual. I thought he'd come to tell Mordred all about how bad I'd been. But he sort of loomed over me, breathing heavily, and then he took me by the shoulder and stood me up and pushed me in front of him back down the corridor.

"Let's have a talk," he said. "In my room."

Back in the classroom he sat me down in front of him. Close up, his face, even in the place where his beard was supposed to be, seemed to have more skin than hair. He smelled a bit cheesy. Not terrible—you wouldn't say he stank—but just not very fresh. I didn't know if he was married, but I doubted it. He had the look of someone who lived alone and didn't have anyone to tell them that they looked stupid or didn't smell too fresh.

"So, what was that all about?" he said. I was surprised by his tone—he sounded sad rather than angry.

"What, sir?"

"You know what I'm talking about, so don't play the idiot. Look, Paul, you're not the kind of kid who usually starts fights. And you're not stupid—I know you're not."

So there was a first time for everything.

"I'm not brainy, sir."

"How do you know? As far as I can see you've never really tried."

I didn't know what to say then, so I just looked down.

"I've noticed you, Paul," continued Mr. Boyle, "just sitting there. I don't know how much you take in, but . . . what's happened to your hair?"

"Nothing, sir. I don't know, sir."

"Is it mixed up with why you were shouting in class?"

"Don't know, sir."

"Don't know much, do you, Paul?"

"I told you I wasn't brainy, sir."

Then I looked at Mr. Boyle, thinking he might be smiling. But he wasn't. He still looked quite sad.

"Can you play chess, Paul?" he said finally.

"Don't know, sir."

"Why not come to chess club to find out?"

Mr. Boyle ran the chess club. It was full of geeks. The kind of kids who brought in thermos flasks of hot soup for their lunch.

I looked up at his face, his wonky glasses, his sparse beard.

"Yes, sir, I might, sir."

There was another pause.

"Maybe see you there then?"

"Yes, sir—just got to get something first."

FIVE

So I went outside and sat by myself on one of the concrete benches. A cold wet wind blew straight off the gypsy field, slapping my face with its clammy hands. It was called the gypsy field because gypsies sometimes camped there, but they hadn't been around for ages, maybe two years. Perhaps there weren't any gypsies left. Just the cold wind, blowing over the grass and picking up the stink from the brown water of the beck.

I wished I'd gone to fetch my parka from the cloakroom. But I didn't want to bump into Boyle. So I pulled up the collar on my school blazer and tried to sit on the tail of it. But it wasn't quite big enough and so the bench was doing a good job of freezing my arse solid. I would have moved to keep warm, but I didn't have anywhere to go. The boys I usually hung around with were playing football, but I didn't feel like it. And, anyway, nobody had asked me to play.

For a second I thought about joining the kids at the chess club, just to keep warm. And maybe it would have been nice to have someone to talk to. Except they'd all be nerds, talking about nerd stuff. *Oh-and-did-you-see-that-really-good-yeah-yeah-documentary-yeah-about-volcanoes-yeah-I-have-the-latest-copy-yeah-of-what-sort-of-hard-drive-do-you-I-wish-I-yeah-what-kind-of-soup.* And I didn't really know how to play chess. I mean, I knew how the pieces moved, but I'd never actually played a game, so I didn't know how to string it all together, how to make sure you didn't get mated in two moves, that sort of thing.

I tried listening to the kids playing, to see if I could single out voices from the general background noise. There were loud shouts of "Pass, pass" from the footballers. And I could hear the high screams from the Year Seven kids, who looked small, even to me. I don't even know what game they were playing. Some kind of tag. Stupid. The girls were all standing about in little groups, and I couldn't hear any noise from them at all, but I could see that some were happy and some were sad and some had a look of fury on their faces, as if they'd just found out that someone had been calling them sluts or something behind their backs.

The only group where boys and girls were together was the freaks. Maybe six of them. They were on the other side of the playground. Some were standing, some were sitting on a bench. Even though everyone was supposed to wear a uniform, they still looked different, as if they were standing in the shadows, while we were all in harsh sunlight.

And somehow you could sense the bad feelings being beamed at them. Mostly it was just that: feelings, a sense that all the other kids in the playground would rather they weren't there. And sometimes it was more than that, like now, when one of the kids playing football deliberately blasted the ball at the group, hitting a girl in the face.

Why does everyone hate the freaks? Well, not everyone. The freaks don't hate the freaks. Actually, even that might not be true. One of the things about them is that they hate themselves. But they don't hate all the freaks, just the individual freak that happens to be them.

I know I shouldn't just call them the freaks, although everyone does. There are other names. You could call them emo. You might even call them indie, or alternative, or scene. But indie and alternative and scene make them sound too cool, too in. They weren't on the inside of anything, except maybe themselves. So emo is probably closer than scene or indie, but freak seems to fit them best of all.

Just being hated by everyone would probably be OK for the freaks. In fact that might be their first choice. But they weren't just hated. Not in our school, anyway. Our school was the kind of school where being hated was only the beginning of things, like with that football blasted into the face of the girl.

The kids who aren't freaks—the freak haters, if you like—come in different flavors. There are some punks, some chavs, some straights, some death metal kids, some glue sniffers, some nerds, and then some who you don't know what they are. And any of them might have a go at a freak. The worst are probably the chavs, who seemed to take the quiet, looking-down way that the freaks had as a direct insult.

No, what am I saying? The chavs aren't the worst. The worst are the droogs, the kids who live to hurt you and take your money. And to them, the freaks are like cattle, to be milked and then slaughtered.

The girl who got hit by the ball, I knew her name. Maddy Bray. She was the only one of them who was in any of my classes. She was standing on the outside of the group of outsiders. It was funny, but when the ball hit her, she didn't move closer to her friends, but farther away, as if she knew that it was somehow her fault, or at least that it was embarrassing. And it was exactly what I'd have done, moving away, trying to disappear.

I watched them for a while, then I saw one of the boys who'd been sitting down stand up and go over to talk to her. I knew his name too. His name was Shane, and I knew it because he was the sort of leader of the freaks. Leader doesn't really get it right, because he didn't tell them what to do or anything. It was more that he was the best at being a freak; he was what they were all aiming at. And even if you hated them and all they stood for, you still had to admit that there was something special about Shane, something cool.

So maybe I should call the freaks Shane's gang, because that's what they were.

Shane smiled and he must have said something funny as well, because Maddy Bray smiled back and nearly laughed, and then she edged a bit closer to the rest of them.

But she stayed on the outside, a watcher, like me.

The beck is at my back. I hear its running water. Except the water in the beck does not run. It limps and staggers, stinking over the scum that oozes at its bottom. But moving. I hear it move. That is bad. Nothing here must be allowed to move. I command the waters to stop.

And they stop.

SIX

And because I was watching, looking over there, right the way across the playground, and not just *looking* there, but *thinking* there too, I didn't see them coming until they were on top of me.

"Look, it's Billy No-mates."

I blinked and made my eyes focus on the pack. Five of them this time—Roth, of course, Bates, Miller, two others.

It wasn't Roth who'd spoken, but Miller, and so he followed it with his hyena laugh.

"Nice haircut," said Roth.

It was the first thing he'd ever said to me directly. He'd probably never even noticed my existence before the stuff in the classroom—the chewing gum, the shout, the chair.

"Yeah," said Bates, "nice haircut. Bit messy, though. Shall I put a bit more gel in it?" And then he began to hawk up a greeny, making a big deal out of it, snorting back from his nose and up from his chest, getting a really big mouthful together.

What happened then was a bit weird. I had my hand in my pocket, and I suppose I'd been playing with them, rubbing my fingers on the metal without thinking about it, without ever knowing with the front bit of my brain that they were there. But the next thing I knew I had them, the scissors. The scissors I'd used to hack the chewing gum out of my hair, and I was holding them out, open so I was gripping the handle and one of the blades, with the other pointing straight at Bates.

I was mad. Mad because of the chewing gum. Mad because I thought he was going to spit on me, spit a thick foul greeny.

They should have laughed at me. It was only scissors. Useless school scissors.

They should have laughed, but they didn't. Bates's eyes went wide and he choked on the phlegm he was getting ready for me, and it sort of dribbled down his chin and onto the front of his school jumper, and then more of it went in a big line, right to the floor, without breaking. I didn't know what to do next. I was feeling stupid, really stupid, standing there holding the scissors, while Bates choked on his slime.

It was Roth who saved me, in a way. Saved me from having to decide what to do next, I mean. He stepped forward, grabbed my wrist and just took the scissors off me, as easily as if I was a baby. His hand was enormous, like a man's.

I thought for sure then that he was going to hit me. Maybe there's something worse that can happen to you than being hit by Roth, but I don't know what it is.

I once saw him have a fight with a Year Eleven kid when he was in Year Nine. Even though the other kid was two years older than him, they were about the same size, Roth being such a monster. And the other kid was cock of his year, not just some nobody. His name was . . . *Compson*, yeah, Compson. Most kids thought Compson was all right. He wasn't really a bully at all, just hard.

I don't know why he had the fight with Roth. Probably thought he had to put him down, because he'd been mouthing off. But as soon as the circle formed in the social club car park, with the two of them in the middle, you could see the fear in his eyes, see that he knew that Roth was too much for him. And I suppose there's a kind of bravery in that, going on with a fight, I mean, even though you know you're going to get your head kicked in.

And he did.

School fights come in different shapes. Sometimes the fighters think they're in a boxing match and dance around each other, with the spectators usually jeering at them and telling them to get stuck in, but they never do, because they're afraid of getting hurt and they're really there to

30

dance, not fight. Or the two will rush straight at each other and grapple together, each one trying to land a punch or a kick, and as long as they stay locked close, then again usually no one gets hurt, because you can't get any power behind a punch when you're together like that, hugging each other.

The worst kind of fights—or the best kind, if watching pain is your idea of fun—are the ones where the two kids hate each other and stand there punching, not caring if they get hit so long as they land a few as well. There aren't many fights like that, and they don't last long, because of the fury of it.

This fight began like that. There was a good crowd around them, the way there always was for a fight, and I think most kids were hoping to see Roth get a spanking, because everyone was scared of him and he always did whatever he wanted.

There was that usual time of intense silence before they started, with Roth staring straight at Compson, and Compson trying to stare back, except you could see he wasn't really focused on Roth, but somewhere behind him. And then there must have been some kind of signal, and they came straight together, and Compson hit Roth twice, quite hard, somewhere up around the forehead. But it was like hitting a truck with a newspaper. Roth didn't even flinch. Hardly even put up his hands.

And when those two punches had no effect, whatever fight there had been in Compson left him, and he ran away, or rather he tried to run away, but the wall of kids bounced him back, with hard laughter. As soon as it was obvious that

Compson was no match for Roth, they'd all changed sides. Nobody likes to back a loser, especially an embarrassing one. He ran round the circle, skittering off the edge of it, looking back over his shoulder at Roth. Roth didn't chase Compson, but just waited awhile, a couple of circuits maybe, and then simply cut him off.

It only took one great scything punch from Roth to lay Compson out flat. The sound was horrible. A sickening soft sound—I mean, the sound of something soft hitting something hard. Almost a squelch, you'd have said. A squelch or a splat. I was standing out of the circle, and so I couldn't see that well, but it was enough, and I heard the sound, and I thought that Roth might have killed Compson with that one big punch, killed him dead.

Roth then did something really bad. Something that had never been seen in our school before.

It took us to a new place. Like the way that the invention of the machine gun took war to a new place.

Compson was on the floor, not even moving. I could just see him through the shifting cage of legs. The punch had got him right in the teeth, and the front of his face had collapsed like a wet bag. He was making a soft slurping noise, so I knew he wasn't dead.

The crowd had gone completely silent and Roth looked slowly around at the kids there, eyeing each one in turn, and no one could stand that black stare and so they would look down or away or shuffle back as though even his look was dangerous.

And when he'd stared everyone out in that slow me-
thodical way, almost like it was a boring job he had to do,
he looked down at the kid lying on the floor, and he sort
of shuffled around inside his trousers—Roth, I mean, not
Compson, who still hadn't moved, and you really would
have thought him dead except for that wet sound coming
from his ruined mouth. And Roth took out his thing—you
know, his *thing*—and he grunted with it in his hands, and
his face became vacant and far away, and then a thick yellow stream of piss came out and splashed down into the face
of Compson.

Well, *that* made him move. He spluttered and rolled,
and then got up onto all fours and looked at Roth, a look
with murder in it, as well as defeat, but Roth stared blandly
back at him, the way you'd look at something reasonably interesting but not really to do with you, and then gave a little half-smile. Compson couldn't hold the look any more
than the watchers in the circle could, and he rolled into a
ball and whimpered, as if to say, *Please don't hit me again.*

Everyone was embarrassed then, and went away. I
went away too, but I looked back, and I thought I'd just see
Compson lying on the ground by himself, because you're
never so alone as when you lose a fight. And he was still
there, but he wasn't alone. Bates and Miller were with him,
kicking him, and stamping on him, and spitting on him, and
I wanted to do something about it, but I was frightened, and
I went home, and anyway it wasn't my business.

And that's what I was remembering when Roth took

my pathetic weapon away from me, the way he'd take sweets from a baby. And I thought some of those things might happen to me now.

But none of those things happened. What happened was that Roth sort of put his big hand against my cheek. I don't know what you'd call it. It was softer than a slap, harder than a touch. And he smiled at me. His teeth were weird. I mean, really weird. They didn't seem to come in different kinds—you know, the front ones different to the back ones; they were all the same, and each one was separate, with a space in between. They were like the unevolved teeth of some ancient animal.

"Look at that," he said, his voice almost warm, almost affectionate. "Will you look at that."

I didn't know what was happening, didn't know what to say.

"Smack him," said Bates. He was bobbing and shuffling like someone needing to go to the toilet.

Roth turned on him. "What?"

Bates was moving even quicker now, foot to foot, up and down, side to side.

"'It 'im. His face, his guts. Make him shit himsen."

Roth waited. A breath, two breaths. His face as bland as putty.

At last: "I think he's all right."

"What? But you saw him . . . saw what he did."

"Shut it."

"Yeah, but—"

And then Roth reached over and grabbed Bates by the scruff of his neck and pulled him closer, giving him a little shake as he did so. Exactly the way you would with a cat. Bates made a high-pitched noise, a sort of squeal.

"Yeah, but what?"

"Nothing, Roth, I was only saying—"

"Well, don't."

"Yeah, yeah, sure."

"What do you reckon, Miller?"

"I reckon he's all right."

"I think he'll do. What do you think, eh?"

Roth was looking at me closely. Not smiling, his face gray putty again. I was so frightened of him I still couldn't say anything.

He wasn't like the other nutters. He was clever and shrewd. It should have meant that you'd be able to understand him better. The others had a kind of unpredictability. Like cats, you didn't know which way they'd turn. But deeper down you could understand them. You could see what they wanted. They were like beasts, and their cravings were the cravings of beasts, and they cowered like beasts cower when they come up against something stronger than them. But Roth was completely incomprehensible. Unlike the beasts, he did everything for a reason, but there were no rules for understanding him. Maybe there was a logic there—in fact I'm sure there was—but it was an alien logic. It was like the Spaniards coming up against the Aztecs. The Aztecs went to war to catch people so they could cut out their hearts to appease their gods, so they'd make it rain and help the crops grow. According to their rules this was all rational. But to the Spaniards it was evil and mad.

I'm not really getting this across. The thing about Roth is that as well as being stronger and harder than anyone else, there was also the fact, the terrible fact, that he was cleverer too. Not clever meaning good at maths or English, but clever meaning that he knew what was happening inside you.

And now he put his heavy arm around my shoulders and drew me away from the others. The weight on me was hard to bear—he was pressing down and squeezing me.

"Don't mind them, they're all right. Just a bit thick," he said, his voice now oddly musical. "You're not thick, though, are you?"

It was funny. The second time today someone had said that.

"Depends what you mean by thick."

Roth smiled more broadly now, showing me those in-human, wide-apart teeth.

"That's what I'm getting at. These jokers would never think like that. You see, I said thick, and you wanted to know what I meant by it. That's 'cos you're thinking"—he pointed to his head—"using this."

And now I'm ashamed to say this part, but I don't want to leave out anything important. When he said that, his voice made soft, intimate, just for me, I felt a glow inside me, a kind of happiness, warmth, peace.

Roth was someone I hated, *should* have hated, more

than any other person. Hated because he was a bad kid, cruel
and vindictive. The kind of kid who would beat another to
a pulp and then piss in his face. The kind of kid who would
get his thicko mates to throw chewing gum in my hair to
help pass the time in a boring geography lesson.

But all he had to do was say those simple words to me,
and I was happy.

What I felt toward him then, for those few seconds,
was love.

"We'll have a chat sometime," said Roth, and then he
wandered away, and the others followed him, because they
had no idea what else to do with their lives.

That left me standing alone, no more able to think for
myself than Bates or Miller. So I gazed into the distance. And
across the playground I saw the group of weird kids, and I noticed that they were looking over in my direction. I didn't
intend it, but my eyes met those of Shane, and he nodded to
me. It was a tiny gesture, one you'd hardly notice, but it was
there. I don't know what he meant by it. Then I took in some
of the others in the group, and for just a second I caught the
eyes of Maddy Bray, and she might have smiled at me, but
then another kid gave her a sort of shove from the side,
which I think was meant to be friendly, but which seemed
wrong for Shane's gang, as they didn't go in much for that
kind of physical kidding around.

And then a bell was ringing and it was time to go.

No one admits to being afraid of death. In books and stories people mock death, and pretend that to die is a small thing. Well, I am afraid of death. Of the death of my body. Of the death of my soul. Of the death coming to find me now, on the gypsy field.

SEVEN

My dad went to my school. Twenty years ago. When he's had a few drinks he tells me what it was like in the olden days. I've made it sound like a rough school now, but back then it was worse. The biggest difference was that the teachers used to hit the kids. All the time. There were three ways of getting hit, my dad said. The basic way was just to get slapped, hard, on the face. Dad said it was OK if they just came up and slapped you, but sometimes you'd be mucking about and a teacher would be behind you, and so you couldn't see the slap coming and it would hit you out of the blue.

The next step up was being hit with the edge of a ruler on the back of the hand. Dad said there was a special ruler in each class and it had a steel edge and was as heavy as a wrench. You had to hold your hand out, knuckles up, and the teachers, if they were cruel, would leave you waiting for a minute, for two minutes, until your hand started to shake. You couldn't stop it, he said. Didn't matter how hard you were. He said sometimes they'd make do with that—the teachers, I mean. Making you tremble. And that was quite bad, but not as bad as when they went through with it, and really let you have it. He said it hurt so much the world would go black for a couple of seconds, and sometimes a kid would wet his pants, but my dad said he never did. It would leave a row of blue lumps, topped by a spot of blood, across your fingers, near where they joined onto your hand. Dad said that you could get it for virtually nothing—for forgetting to bring something to school, for not being in a straight line, for smiling when you should have a face of stone. For having a face of stone when you should be smiling.

But the top of the range was the cane—a long whippy stick of bamboo. Even then there were variations. Backside or hand. Dad said that getting the cane on the hand actually hurt the most, but it somehow wasn't half as bad as having to bend over a chair, feeling as helpless as a worm on the pavement, and taking it on the arse. Dad said that kids always boasted when they got caned on the hand, but when it was the arse, they just shut up, and nothing could get them to talk about it.

They can't hit you now. The teachers, I mean. You can tell that some of them want to, some of them *really* want to. You can see their jaws working in little circles with the effort of not hitting you.

But they can do other things. One of the things they do is humiliate you. If you shame and degrade a kid, you know the other kids will do the rest for you. For some reason the teachers never seem to bother much with the hard kids, the troublemakers. The ones they hate are the quiet ones. Not just any of the quiet ones, but the quiet ones who aren't interested in them, the ones who are always looking into themselves.

The lost kids. The freaks. Yeah, you got it: Shane and his gang.

I never quite got why the teachers hated them. Maybe it's because people don't like it when they aren't in on the secret, and the freaks went around like they had it—I mean, the Big Secret, the one we all want to know.

The best example of a teacher who loved humiliation, who relished and ate it like some sickly delicacy—Turkish delight, or marzipan—was Mrs. Eel. After break, after my talk with Roth, I had French with her. Mrs. Eel taught French to the kids who weren't very good at French, and I think that pissed her off.

You learned pretty quick to be careful around her.

A big mistake was calling her Miss—rather than Mrs.—Eel. The way she'd react, well, you'd think you'd called her Mad Bitch or something. Another mistake was to find whatever exercise she had set too easy or too hard. If you made a mistake like that, she would talk quietly to begin with, so you strained to hear what she was saying, and then suddenly she'd scream, and her eyes would be insane, and sometimes a little bit of spit would fly out.

Other days she'd just be bored, and then she'd pick on someone for no reason at all, some pathetic loner, some harmless wisp of a boy, or a shy girl struggling to come to terms with her body, or a fat kid, or one raddled with acne.

Having found herself a victim, she would spend the entire lesson mauling him or her with a feline grace it was hard not to admire. And the worst thing was that she would draw the rest of us into it.

I went into the class with my head down. Mrs. Eel was sitting behind her desk with her back to the class and her feet up on the windowsill. That was bad news.

The class was all right, meaning there weren't any kids there to be scared of, just Mrs. Eel. But there was one thing about the class. I sort of said it earlier. That girl was in it, the one who got hit by the football.

Getting hit by the ball was typical of Maddy Bray. She was unlucky. The most unlucky thing about her was how she looked. I mean, how she looked combined with her name. Bray isn't a beautiful name, and maybe someone called Bray is always going to get some stick. But if you're called Bray and you have a long, horsy face, well, then you're in trouble.

You know that thing you can do, when you have to put everyone you know, or everyone who comes through a door,

42

into one of two groups—currant bun or horse. Currant bun means round face. Horse means long face. Well, Maddy was definitely horse.

But that makes her sound worse than she was. Because horse can go either way. I mean, sometimes horse can be bad, but sometimes it can be good. Currant bun is usually in the middle somewhere. I don't think you could say that Maddy was beautiful to look at. But there was something about her face that made you want to look at it, that made you want to stare. And I don't mean the way you would at something terrible, some really bad birthmark. It was just the feeling that you could never quite get to the bottom of her face. Sorry, that sounds stupid. I don't know what I mean, really, except that her face was something I found it hard not to look at.

Like I said, Maddy was in the Shane gang, but she wasn't that good at it—being a freak, that is. She never got the look quite right. She was tight where she should have been baggy, and baggy where she should have been tight. And she knew this—knew that she wasn't there—but didn't know enough to put it right. She was so conscious of her failings that she spoke to almost no one, and moved silently, like a shadow, through the school, looking at nothing but her own big feet.

Maddy was clever, or at least she was in the top set for most things, so I don't know how she ended up in Eel's class with me. I suppose you can't be good at everything. But the trouble was that even if she wasn't great at French, she was better than the rest of us, and that was a dangerous thing with Mrs. Eel. And so Mrs. Eel loathed her. Someone who knew all about what goes on inside other people's heads might say that she hated her because she feared that she might be a little bit like her, and that can be reason enough for hating if you're afraid of what you might be. And someone with a simpler view of things might say that she hated her because she was a hating person, and that asking why Mrs. Eel hated Maddy Bray was like asking why a kid likes the taste of sugar.

All year I'd winced and squirmed as Mrs. Eel tormented Maddy. She'd make her read out the most difficult passages, things that no one else in the class would have got anywhere with. And Maddy would struggle through, with Mrs. Eel not just correcting her every word, but actually laughing at her, laughing in her face.

And there were other, slyer tricks.

There was a kid in the class called Mark Hampson who stank of piss. I don't know why he stank of piss. He didn't look dirty. Usually looked quite smart, in fact. Maybe he was a bed wetter or something. Mrs. Eel made us sit in alphabetical order. Quite a few teachers did it, as a way of making sure you couldn't sit next to your friends. About halfway through the first term, by which time she'd worked out both that Hampson stank and that she hated Maddy Bray, she changed the system so that it was based on your first name, which meant Maddy and Mark were together. It was little touches like this that made Mrs. Eel special. Attention to detail, I suppose you'd call it.

I was sitting at the back of the class, keeping my profile low. Mrs. Eel had written up an exercise on the white board. She hadn't even spoken to us, but just waved at the board. My mind wasn't on the class—it never was. But now I had more to think about than usual. The chewing gum in my hair; the strange talk with Roth.

Then, out of the corner of my eye, I saw that Mrs. Eel was starting to fidget, leaning her chin first on her right hand, then on her left. I guessed that this meant trouble, and I slipped further down in my chair. And then I saw Mrs. Eel fix her gaze on Maddy Bray. Maddy had finished the exercise, and had made the mistake of putting her pen down.

A little smile flickered across Mrs. Eel's mouth, like a cockroach skittering across the lino.

"So, finished already, *Maddy*," she said, her words hardly a whisper. But she'd managed to make the word Maddy sound like something you'd scrape off your shoe.

"Yes, Miss . . . Mrs. Eel."

That was lucky. Sort of.

"It would seem we're not really stretching you in this class, are we?"

"No, Mrs. . . . I mean, yes, Mrs. Eel."

"Perhaps we're boring you?"

The rest of the class were alert now, aware that something was happening. And I sensed the general relief that it was happening to this outsider, this half-emo girl.

"Bray?"

"Yes, Mrs. Eel?"

"Do you know the French for 'donkey'?"

"No, Mrs. Eel."

"Do you know the French word for the sound a donkey makes?"

"No, Mrs. Eel."

"Can you make a sound like a donkey?"

"No, Mrs. Eel."

"Yes you can, Bray."

"Please, Mrs. Eel, don't."

"Make a sound like a donkey, Bray."

"Please . . ."

"Bray, Bray. What does a donkey look like, Bray?"

"Don't know, Mrs. Eel."

"Look in the mirror, Bray."

All sounds a bit lame? You forget the power of humiliation. You don't realize what a gift this was to the class arseholes. But more than that, all of us were sucked in by the teacher's dominance and contempt. The class was half loving it. It was a Christian thrown to the lions, and we were the people of Rome, cheering on each bite. Except there wasn't any cheering, just silent glee.

I couldn't stand it. There were kids in the class who might have deserved that kind of treatment, but not poor long-faced Maddy Bray. And I think I still had some leftover anger from what had happened to me earlier. Anger mixed up with the embarrassment of not having done anything about it, and then of feeling overpowered by Roth.

If I'd been a different kind of person, I might have been

able to say something funny or clever to make it stop. But that's not me. I'm not funny or clever. So I did something else. I didn't know what it was going to be until I started doing it, although the truth is it was something I'd daydreamed about before, as a way of escaping. I'd even looked it up on the Internet, seen some photos and even a couple of short video sequences.

So I fell off my chair. Then I started shaking. Really shaking. I didn't have any way of making my mouth foam, and drooling seemed way too gross, so I kept my mouth clamped shut, like that was part of it. My arms were rigid by my sides, and I tried to make the shaking seem like some terrible irresistible force that I was fighting against.

I sensed the commotion all around me. There were screams and shouts and the noises people make when they're faintly disgusted but also fascinated. I heard Mrs. Eel, her voice high with indignation and anger. I'd ruined it for her, ruined her fun with Maddy Bray.

"Get back, let me see," she said. "Has he done this before?"

"No, miss."

"What did you say?"

"No, Mrs. Eel. Really sorry, Mrs. Eel. It was him freaking out like that."

Then I thought I'd done enough. I stopped twitching and just lay there.

"He's stopped, Mrs. Eel."

"I can see that, you stupid girl."

"Peter, Peter, can you hear me?"

"His name's Paul, Mrs. Eel."

There was a small silence. I imagined the look that Mrs. Eel was sending out.

"Paul! Paul!"

I felt her hands on my shoulders. She began to shake me. That probably wasn't the recommended treatment for an epileptic.

I groaned.

"Mrs. Eel. We should put him in the recovery position."

I recognized the voice. It was Maddy Bray's.

"Well, go on then, girl."

I was on my back. I felt new, softer hands on me, rolling me over, moving my legs. I felt her breath on my cheek. I opened my eyes. Her face was so close it covered up everything. When she saw my eyes, she looked startled for a second. And then at long last, after all these years, I did the right thing, did a cool thing. I winked. And Maddy Bray smiled quickly back at me. She shared my secret. She knew what I'd done.

EIGHT

I was in the sick bay. The sick bay was a horrible little room where you got sent if you puked or had a headache. There was a kind of bed to lie down on, a special sort of medical bed covered in black plastic, and a bucket to throw up in, and another bucket full of sand. There was also a dummy person in there. It didn't have any legs, just the head and the middle bit with the arms attached. I don't know what it was for—maybe teaching about the human body or for learning the kiss of life or something. But someone had drawn a dick going into its mouth. I say "it," but it was really a she. You could tell from the head, which still had long hair, although a lot of it had fallen out. They'd tried to clean it off—the dick, I mean—but you could still see it. So now she just lived in the corner of the sick bay. She looked a bit sad. Yeah, a bit freaky.

I was lying on the bed, not really knowing what to do with myself. The vinyl covering of the bed had burn holes and tears in it, and I really wanted to pick at them.

Mrs. Eel had obviously been glad to see the back of me. I don't think she liked the idea of someone dying in her classroom, even though by then I'd recovered—I mean, pretended to recover. I even climbed back onto my chair. But Mrs. Eel said I had to go to see the school secretary, and that was that.

It was the secretary, who was called Miss Bush, who sent me to the sick bay. She asked me if it had happened before, and I said it had, quite often, and it was always fine after a few minutes. Then she'd told me to lie down and stay quiet. I said that, really, I was all right now, but she seemed to think that as long as she got me to lie down in the sick bay then she'd done her duty, showed that she was caring and all that. Probably covered herself against getting sued. Lying down and staying quiet was as far as medical treatment went at our school. I'm pretty sure that if you turned up with your head under your arm, Miss Bush would still tell you to lie down and stay quiet.

There was a creak, and I looked over at the sick-bay door. A head peeped round. I didn't know what to expect, and if I'd had a hundred guesses I would never have got it right. It was Shane, the leader of the freaks.

"Can I come in?" he asked in a soft voice. "I mean, I know how ill you are, and I don't want to, like, put back your recovery."

He said it with a completely straight face, but he got across the message that he was joking. It made me laugh.

"Did you bring me any grapes?"

"Nah, just monkey nuts and hard-boiled eggs."

I didn't understand that, but I knew it must be a joke, so I laughed again.

"I heard what you did. Maddy told me. That was cool."

"Yeah, well, I couldn't just . . . couldn't just, you know."

"Well, most kids would have just . . . you know."

Again there was a kind of mockery in what Shane was saying—I mean, making fun of my clumsy words—but it didn't bite, because it was like, even though it was me he was sort of mocking, he also seemed to be on the same side as me. As though we were both taking the piss, and both having the piss taken out of us at the same time.

"Your name's Paul Varderman, isn't it?"

I nodded.

"My name's Shane."

"I know. I think everyone knows who you are."

"Why's that?"

"That thing with Frisco."

The thing with Frisco was famous. Frisco was the scary little Irish PE teacher who only spoke in two ways: a sinister, quiet voice and a bellow. One rainy day when the year was all in together for PE, Frisco tried to get Shane to do something—can't even remember what it was now—using his quiet voice, and Shane said, "I'm sorry, sir, you'll have to speak up," and then, when Frisco screamed at him, he said, "There's really no need to shout." It all sounds a bit tame now, but it was fantastic at the time, and no one had ever dared talk back to Frisco like that, even if everything Shane said was actually quite polite. Frisco marched him off into the room where all the gear was stored—beanbags and hoops, that sort of thing—and we all heard more shouting, and a bumping sound, and then a scream from Frisco of "YOUR HEAD IS GOING TO BOUNCE OFF THAT WALL!" And then Shane walked out of there as if nothing had happened at all, not a bit ruffled or bothered, but Frisco came out looking like he'd been the one who'd bounced around the walls, with his hair and eyes all wild. It was like Frisco was a storm and Shane was a lighthouse. A lighthouse that smiled.

It's hard to get across how great that was. It was a little victory for the kids against the teachers, but not the usual one, where hard kids intimidate the soft teachers. There are plenty of victories like that and they don't count for anything. No, it's worse than that: they make everyone's life a bit shittier. This was different: this was a kid standing up to a bully, but in a way that you just had to describe as cool.

It's one of the reasons the hard kids never went after

Shane. Everyone still hated the freaks, but if Shane was around, they didn't bother them as much.

"Mrs. Eel really is an old bitch," I said. "Well, not that old."

"But a bitch. Yeah, Maddy said. And, well, guess what, she's here."

"Mrs. Eel?"

"Ha ha. No, Maddy. She just didn't want to come straight in."

I felt myself begin to blush. Shane smiled at me. Then Maddy's face peered round the door.

"Hi," she said, looking as awkward as I felt. "I just wanted to say thanks." Then she looked down at the floor. She was still half in and half out.

"It was nothing, really." My heart was pounding and my voice sounded weird in my ears. But I made myself carry on. "Anyway, at least it got me out of the lesson."

"Yeah."

"Yeah."

After a bit of a pause Shane said, "We're meeting up at my place after school, if you want to come round."

"Who's 'we'? You mean the fr—?"

"The freaks?"

"I didn't mean . . ."

"Hey, sure, you've probably got something better to do. Anyway, see you around."

"No, no," I said, trying not to sound too desperate, "I've

got nothing on. I'd really like to, you know, come round and hang out. Where do you live?"

"Up in Halton. Manston Gardens. Know it?"

"Yeah, I've been up there. Posh houses."

"Not really. After tea then, anytime. I'm number seven."

Then there was a bit of confusion, because Mr. Boyle was trying to get in, which meant squeezing past Maddy, and bumping into Shane, and putting his glasses straight, which was all quite a lot for him to manage.

"We'll see you," said Shane, and he and Maddy disappeared.

"Thought I'd stop by," said Mr. Boyle. "Feeling better?"

"Yes, sir, fine, sir."

"OK, good, good, good." Then a pause, before he went on, stumbling over his words. "Is this anything to do with what happened earlier?"

"How do you mean, sir?"

"I thought you might have been, er, agitated. You know, in a state."

I felt a bit crap about that. I mean, Mr. Boyle being nice, taking time out to see how I was, trying to join things up, when I was just faking it.

"No, sir, it just happened. No biggie."

"Well, that's good. And nice to see your friends dropping in on you."

Friends. Well, I couldn't really call them friends. But, yeah, it was good.

"And maybe we'll see you in chess tomorrow? They're not so bad, you know."

"Who do you mean, sir?"

"The chess nerds."

That made me laugh.

"No, sir."

No! I did not concentrate. I thought about death as a word, and not about death as a thing, the thing coming closer. I check back to the knife. Is it nearer? Yes, of course it is. The ghost trail of outlines shows that the knife has moved, carrying the boy with it. The water behind me has surged. Hearts have beaten, blood has flowed. The end is closer.

NINE

I stayed in the sick bay all afternoon. I think Miss Bush had forgotten I was there, and no one else looked in. I could have gone home. I could have gone back to class. It was metalwork in the afternoon, and I don't mind that. I'd been making a car out of cast-off bits of metal, just the crap lying around, and Mr. Robinson thought it was quite good. Mr. Robinson was one of the teachers who was nice if you stayed on his good side. But if you did something wrong—say, messed up on the lathe or didn't pay attention when he was telling us about safety—then he could turn savage.

So I could have done either of those, but I was liking it there in the quiet room, even if it smelled a bit of old sick. And if I'd gone home, I'd only have had to explain things to Mum.

I liked waiting to hear the bells at the end of each period, and the other sounds—the rush of feet, the loud voices. Usually the space in between lessons is a time of danger, when someone would smash you into a corridor wall, or trip you up, or take your bag and fling it down the stairwell. But I was safe from all that. And it was pleasant to think about going round to hang out with Shane and his friends. Pleasant, but also a bit scary. Whenever I tried to imagine what we'd do together, everything broke down. I didn't know them at all, didn't know what they'd want to talk about. I was always shy with new people. Sometimes with new people I'd clam up. Sometimes I'd say too much. There were all kinds of ways it could go wrong. They might think I was boring. Or I might come out with stuff they thought was stupid.

I decided I wouldn't go.

No, I had to go.

Things weren't right in my life, I knew that. Ever since coming to this school things had been going wrong. No, not going *wrong*, going *off*. Like something forgotten at the back of the fridge. I didn't know how or why, but I had an instinct that Shane was a way out of things, a way back from the edge.

So, when the end-of-day bell rang, I waited a few

minutes just for things to calm down outside, and then got up from the sick bed and set off home.

There were still a few kids messing about in the playground by the back entrance. I usually went out the front way, because there were more teachers around and it felt safer. But I was in a hurry, and the back way was quicker.

They jumped me a couple of meters outside the gates. They'd been hiding behind the wall of the social club. It was Miller and Bates. They grabbed an arm each and dragged me over the grass and down toward the beck. The beck is the stream that flows past the school. It's dirty and it stinks and you get rats there. My dad says it was worse when he was a kid, and that if you fell in it you'd die—not from drowning, because it wasn't deep enough (unless someone held you down), but by being poisoned.

I knew more or less what was in store for me. They were going to chuck me in—something like that. I thought it was because Bates wanted to get revenge—I mean, for me pulling the stupid scissors on him, and it must have been frustrating that Roth didn't smack me earlier. Weird how Roth had protected me. But he wasn't here now, and these two were going to make me sorry I'd even thought about standing up to them.

Except Roth *was* there. I saw him when we got closer. There were steep banks down to the water, so he'd been hidden from where I was. He had his back to us, and he was sitting on a coat—not his, he was wearing a leather jacket, so it must have belonged to Bates or Miller. I'm not really into fashion, but I could tell that Roth's jacket wasn't that cool. Wasn't cool at all, really. It looked tough, though. I mean, tough like an armadillo skin.

"Got him, Roth," said Miller. "He come out late. Been hiding somewhere. Little poof."

"I wasn't hiding," I said. Then Bates twisted the arm he was holding behind my back. It hurt. But I didn't cry out. It would take more than that to make me cry out.

But I was afraid. If it had just been Miller and Bates I would have known what was in store for me. Like I said, they'd have pushed me in the water. Chucked bricks at me to keep me there for a bit. Then they'd have run off laughing at the great joke of it all. I could endure that. I'd endured worse. But with Roth you just didn't know, and I felt my guts turn soft inside me.

He turned round to look over his shoulder. He was so massive the movement was awkward, as if the muscles got in the way.

"What you playing at?"

I thought he was talking to me, and I was trying to think of an answer when Miller said, "Nothing, just like you said, asked him to—"

"Dunt look to me like you asked him. Looks like you told him."

"Yeah, we told him but—"

"Let him go."

He was facing forward again now, looking at the water's bubbling brown scum.

"Come here."

A hand at my back pushed me hard.

"Have a sit down."

The grass was wet. There was no question of sharing the coat. I felt the wetness seep through my trousers.

"Sorry about them nutters. I just said ask you to come along for a little chat."

"It's all right. They don't bother me."

He turned toward me, giving me a full, black-eyed stare. "Maybe they should."

Was that a threat? Or was he saying I should stand up to them more? Up to his own henchmen?

I shrugged. This was getting weirder. What did he want with me? Part of me still thought that this was a setup, that any second he was going to join in with Miller and Bates and chuck me in the water, or maybe just smash my face in. Then I saw that Miller and Bates had wandered off along the bank. There was a narrow path—not planned, just made by thousands of kids' feet. Miller had a long stick and was jabbing it into the mud at the bottom of the beck, stirring up old filth. Clouds of the greenish muck floated, billowing down to where we were sitting, bringing a stink like some foul mix of eggs and shit.

"I wonder about them two," Roth said, in a friendly, confiding sort of way.

"You're right to," I replied.

Roth chuckled. "I couldn't trust them with anything important. Couldn't trust them to tell me what they had for breakfast unless they were still eating it."

That made me laugh. I felt myself getting sucked into something. Something over my head.

"And the thing is," he said, turning those black eyes on me once more, "I've got a little job I need doing."

"A job?" I smiled weakly.

"Yeah, nothing much. A little delivery."

"What is it?"

"Don't panic." Roth slapped me on the back. "Not heavy. Just stick it in your bag."

It was then that I noticed for the first time that there was a parcel on the ground next to Roth. It was the size of a shoe box, wrapped in brown paper and then covered all over again in Scotch tape. There was something slightly insane about the Scotch tape. It was everywhere, wrapped round and round the package like bandages round a mummy.

"I'm not sure I can—"

"Look, here's something to make it worth your while."

He felt in his pocket and held out a tenner. I didn't reach out to take it from his hand. The thing with Roth was that when he was mad, his face did the opposite of what you'd expect. Rather than showing the lines of rage, his face would become more blank. For a second that happened now, the human lines on his face smoothing away to an implacable, machine soullessness. But only for a second. Then he grinned, and shoved the note into the breast pocket of my blazer.

"Good lad," he said.

Had my face betrayed me? Told him, in response to his own, unspoken threat, that I would do whatever he wanted? I don't know, but I think that if he'd really tried to force me, I might have resisted, or might have said yes, and then thrown the package away. But his assumption that I'd agreed, his acceptance of it as natural, as inevitable, destroyed my will to resist. I told you Roth was deep.

But I had one last, feeble go at refusing.

"Can't you get one of them to take it?"

"Look at them," he said, and I followed his line of vision. Bates had hold of the stick, and had dredged up some of the weed and slime from the bottom and was waving it at Miller, the two of them whooping and laughing. "A cretin and a nigger. Too dumb to fart and walk at the same time."

The casual brutality of Roth's language stunned me, and I hated it, and hated him. I didn't think even Roth would say "nigger" like that, as if it was a word like "idiot," one you could drop into a conversation. But it was another part of his plan to draw me in. For a second I was part of the inner circle, just me and Roth. The safest part of the hurricane is at the eye.

And hell has its circles.

And then my voice said:

"Where do you want it taken?"

That was it: I was committed.

"That's ma boy. Up to the sports ground. The one in Temple Moor. You can take the bus up."

"But all the Temple Moor kids hang out there."

"Very, ah, *astute*."

"But they'll see me. . . ."

Temple Moor High School was nearly as rough as ours. And there had always been trouble between us. Sometimes it was war. Sometimes an uneasy peace.

"Look, it's all cool with them. In fact it's one of them you'll be dropping this off with. Black kid. Called Goddard. They call him Goddo. It's something he wants."

"Like what?"

"Seriously, *Paul*, you don't really want to know. Just a package."

I could guess.

Drugs.

I felt sick.

But there was no way out now. Well, there was a way out, but I couldn't take it. I was already too far down the path.

Drugs weren't that big at our school. A while back there had been a serious problem with glue and solvents, but one kid died with a can of lighter fluid up his nose, and that kept things quiet for a while. A few of the older kids talked about dope and speed, but I'd never heard of anything worse than that.

"You look a bit peaky. I'm telling you, there's nothing

64

to worry about. And it's one little favor. After this, you and me, we're mates, all right?"

I didn't want to be mates with Roth. I didn't want to hang around with him and the nutters like Bates and Miller. But I did want something from him. Something hard to put your finger on. I'd felt it already today. It was as if Roth put out fields—I mean, like radiation or something. And there were two different kinds. There was the one that killed you, the death field, and the one that protected you. If you were in that field, then you were OK, you were safe. Safe from anything. But it was really hard to know sometimes where one field ended and the other began.

He handed me the package. It was heavier than I thought. It's funny. Sometimes when things are heavier than you expect, it's a good feeling. And this should have been a good feeling now, because surely this was too heavy to be drugs. It weighed as much as a cricket ball, more maybe.

"When shall I take it?"

"Now."

"Now? But . . . but I've got to go somewhere else."

"That can wait."

"No, I . . ." But I didn't carry on, because I could easily get from Temple Moor to Halton. It just meant I couldn't go home first. And I knew that I didn't have the strength to tell a convincing lie to Roth.

And so again I asked him:

"Tell us what it is, Roth."

And Roth put his hand at the back of my neck and squeezed, and pulled me toward him at the same time. The pain wasn't that bad, but I knew it was a message, and the message was: *I can hurt you whenever I want to*.

"Ask me that again and you'll find out," he said, and that filled me with more dread than anything so far.

And then he showed me his teeth. This close I could see the flat tops. They looked like they'd been worn down, worn smooth. *I'll grind your bones to make my bread*. It came into my head like that.

"Get going, or you'll miss him."

I nodded, and began to get up. And then Roth pulled me back down again.

"But just to be on the safe side," he said, in a low voice, "you'd better take something. For self-defense."

Then, keeping eye contact, he put something metal in my hand. I looked down.

It was the scissors.

I heard wild laughter. Miller and Bates had appeared from nowhere to enjoy the joke.

TEN

I went to the bus stop. I could have walked—it's only twenty minutes—but I was afraid that Roth might be watching, and he'd told me to take the bus. There were a few other kids there, larking around. No one I knew. I was daydreaming. Thinking about Shane. Thinking about Maddy. Sometime in between seeing her get hit by the ball and her visit to me in the sick bay I'd realized something. Something that was probably there all along, but I'd never acknowledged it. I liked her. I liked her a lot.

You probably think it's weird that I liked Maddy, after

what I said about her. Not exactly cool. Not exactly pretty. But she had something. Something strange, like she heard secret voices or saw things that other kids couldn't see. That's making it sound worse. Maybe it was just that I thought she was a bit like me.

There was a loud honk, yanking me out of my thoughts. I looked up, already knowing what I'd see. It was my dad, leaning out of the window of his truck cab. I felt my face burn.

"Where you off to, son?"

"Just up the hill, Dad. I'm . . . I'm meeting some friends up on Temple Moor."

"Hop in. I'll give you a lift."

"It's all right, Dad, I'll get the bus."

"What for? Money wasted. Get in."

He opened the door for me, and I climbed up. The cab was hot and it smelled of my dad—not foul, but a bit sweaty. I opened the window, and the truck juddered and chugged into motion.

"Who are these friends then?"

"Just some kids."

"But why are you meeting up there? You've got to watch yourself."

"Yeah, Dad, I know."

"Did I ever tell you about the big fight up there when I was your age?"

"Yeah, Dad."

"It was the whole school, virtually. Streaming up there

like an army. You see, one of their kids had nicked a bird off one of ours. Over nothing, really."

"I know, Dad."

"All our hard kids were there. And I'm telling you, back then, when I say hard, I mean hard. Not like now."

"You've told me, Dad."

"Funny thing is, though, we took a right spanking that day. We were on their patch. And Temple Moor has always been a bigger school. We got surrounded. I wasn't even supposed to be fighting, just watching. But some of the little kids got mixed up in it, and I had to dive in to help them."

"I know, Dad."

"Well, someone had to."

He'd told me the story a million times. Me and anyone else who'd listen. About how he shepherded the little kids, protecting them from the Temple Moor meat-heads. How everyone said he saved their lives, even though he'd just saved them from getting a kicking. How even the Temple Moor kids nodded at him afterward. I was sick of it, to be honest.

"But it's all right now, Dad. We're not fighting them anymore."

"So what are you doing up there?"

"Like I said, just meeting some mates. Drop me here, will you, Dad."

"OK, son." He ruffled my hair. "Stay out of trouble, eh?"

"See you, Dad."

I cut through the shops at the top of the hill. There was a pound store where you could buy anything shit for a pound—shit batteries, shit biscuits, shit baby clothes. And there was a liquor store where the guy stood behind a grille so you couldn't rob him. It was the first one of those they had in our town, and people used to come just to look at it. It was like something in an American film, so people thought it was kind of cool.

Past the shops, and soon you were in what looked a lot like countryside, although you could always see the shadow of the big council estate that looped around one side of it. We'd done the history of this place at school. The land was given to the Knights Templar in twelve something. That's why it was called Temple Moor. They had a big farm, making money to help them fight the Saracens in the Holy Land. Then the Templars got slaughtered, not by the Saracens but by the kings in Europe who wanted their money, and I can't remember what happened to the land, until hundreds of years later someone built a big house, and it's still there, kind of beautiful. You can go round it and look at the chairs and beds of the rich people who used to live there.

But I didn't have to go near the big house to get to the sports ground. I knew it quite well, because we always had our school sports day there. You probably wouldn't have guessed it, but the best time I ever had at school happened on sports day. I don't know why, but Frisco made me volunteer to do the triple jump. I'm OK at sport, nothing special. Not in any school teams, but I can run. Frisco said, "Any volunteers for triple jump?" and then, "Right, you, Varderman," before anyone had put their hand up.

I'd never done the triple jump. None of us had. It was a new thing. I think Frisco brought it in just because it was quite hard to get right, and he wanted to see some of the kids fall on their faces in front of the whole school. It was a sunny day. I was against all the really sporty kids in the year. I did a couple of practice runs. The first time I messed up, stumbled, fell. The next time I went slowly, but got each stage right: hop, skip, jump. I didn't get very far, but I could do it—you know, basically do it.

Because the day was running late we were only allowed one jump in the competition, which was stupid. It was probably all part of Frisco's plan. And it nearly worked. Every jump was a no-jump. Kids stepped over the board, or got the stages wrong, or didn't bother with the stages at all, but just took a big leap, thinking that would be OK.

And then I came along. Yeah, I just did it, easy as anything. Not many people were watching as there were other events on at the same time. A kid called Franklin punched the side of my head because I'd beat him. But I didn't care. It was the only time I ever came first in anything at school. And now nothing can change that.

Wait. I never said the knife wouldn't move. I said it could never reach me. The distance will halve, the time will halve. Infinity does not require that there is no movement. In fact it demands that there *is*. The plan is working. I am safe. The knife will never get here. We are safe.

ELEVEN

I saw them hanging round some benches near the changing rooms and clubhouse. Six—no, seven of them. They looked pretty mean to me, although that could just have been because of the history.

I could tell the second the gang saw me: the excitement went through their bodies, jolting each one.

Here comes some fun, they thought.

I took the box out of my bag and held it out in front of me as I approached them. I was trying to look purposeful, but not dangerous. Ha! That was funny. As if I could ever be a danger to them. But I wanted at least to look like I was there for a reason, and not just like some aimless kid, ripe for robbing of his pocket money.

The gang had stopped talking among themselves, and now watched me, their stares openly hostile. I was frightened. I tried to think of my dad, tried to think what he'd have done. But thinking about my dad never really helped me. Somehow thinking of his strength always made me feel weaker. Imagining his courage made me want to hide.

About ten meters away from them I stopped and shouted out: "I've got something for Goddo."

My voice chose that moment to crack, and it came out as a squeaking croak. At least that broke the tension, and they laughed.

Too hard.

Too long.

"Hear that, Goddo, he's got something for you," one of the kids said at last, copying my squeak. The laughter swelled again. It was impossible to know how this would turn out.

Something about Goddo reassured me. He was a head taller than the other kids, but he had the kind of face that fell easily into a smile.

"He better bring it here then," he said.

His tone wasn't unfriendly, and the words still had that smile or the promise of a smile behind them. I was struck by the difference between him and Roth. There was never a time when Roth wasn't asserting his dominance over you, letting you know that he was the master and you were clay. Goddo seemed less concerned with making the world bow to his will. But it might have been an act. After all, I was still far enough away to have a chance of escaping if I ran for it, so he could just have been trying not to scare me off.

But the truth is that I was more scared of Roth than of any of these kids, and I wasn't going to run. I walked the rest of the way to the group.

"It must be your birthday," one of the gang said. A scrawny kid with spiky hair. He looked like something spat out by a dog.

I stretched out my arm to Goddo and he took the package.

"Who's it from?" he asked.

"Roth."

"Roth?" he said, looking puzzled.

I hadn't thought for a moment that he wouldn't know who Roth was. It was like not knowing who Jesus was, or the Queen.

Then he twigged.

"Oh, you mean that ape-man?"

The others laughed. The spiky-haired kid did an ape walk, rolling along on bandy legs, his knuckles dragging on the ground.

I didn't like that. I don't mean calling Roth an ape-man; I mean the fact that Goddo didn't seem to know what this was all about. Although I wasn't exactly delighted at the idea of running drugs, I thought at least it was a deal between them, something they'd agreed on. That's where my safety lay.

Goddo weighed the package in his hands. "Quite heavy. What is it?"

"Dunno. I'm just the messenger." At least I'd got the sentence out without squeaking.

"Open it up," said the spiky-haired kid, pulling at Goddo's arm.

"What do you think I'm doing?" replied Goddo, shrugging him off. He picked at the Scotch tape. "Give us your knife, Mickey."

A knife. I felt another surge of unease.

Then Mickey, the scrawny kid, took out a Swiss Army knife. I felt oddly reassured by that. Yeah, a penknife can kill you, but it's not exactly the weapon of choice for a gangsta. What if you opened up the corkscrew or nail file instead of a blade?

Goddo found one of the shorter blades and cut through the wrapping. The brown paper eased open, and Goddo let it fall. The box inside had a picture of a heart on top.

"I was wrong, it's Valentine's day," said Mickey.

He was obviously the comedian of the group. But this time the others were too engrossed in the box to laugh.

It was then that I really should have run, while they were checking out the package. Even if they'd bothered chasing me, they might not have caught me.

Goddo had been smiling, but now his face changed.

He moved the box to one hand and looked at the fingers of the other, touching them together as if there was something sticky on them. Then he held the box up to eye level and peered underneath.

"Something leaking," he said, almost to himself.

Then he opened the box.

And dropped it.

Mickey let out a scream, and the rest of the gang shouted and stepped back.

Again I should have bolted. I'd have made it, I know I would. But I was hypnotized by the box, caught by my desire to see what it contained. So I moved forward rather than away, and looked at what Goddo had dropped.

The box was empty. Its contents had rolled out. For a second I couldn't see what it was. I moved closer still. And then I saw.

It was a head.

A dog's head.

Black and brown fur. The shocking pink tongue, lolling. Dull eyes, staring. White teeth. Blood thickly oozing.

Looked like a pit bull. Except a pit bull never appeared so vulnerable. Or so dead.

"Suzie."

Goddo spoke the word. And then he did the shocking thing. He picked up the head he had let fall from the box, brought it to his face and kissed the black lips.

I must have made some sort of noise then, because they all turned and looked at me. I think they'd forgotten I was there. Too late now, I tried to run, but they were on me. Two grabbed my arms and one held me by the hair, pulling my head back. Mickey stood in front of me. Somehow he'd got the knife back from Goddo. He pointed the blade at my exposed neck. They were all shouting and the world seemed to spin and reel in my eyes.

"Slit his throat," someone said, one of the kids holding me.

"Yeah, bleed him."

"You saw what he did. I'm gonna cut his head off. Send it back to them. Head for a head."

The kids holding my arms pulled and twisted them further behind my back, and I felt the hand in my hair circle closer to my scalp, and then yank back. I gasped with the pain. But I never took my eyes off the knife. Mickey put the blade to my throat and pressed. I felt it cut into me, felt a trickle of warm blood run like a tear.

"Aw, baby cry, baby cry."

"Leave him."

Goddo again. I felt a swell of pure gratitude toward him. He pushed Mickey out of the way, and my gratitude turned to horror. He was holding the head. His eyes had gone. He looked mad. I mean mad crazy, not mad angry.

He put his face close to mine, then raised the dog's head.

"Why?"

"I swear I didn't know. Roth . . . it was a trick . . . against me. I'm not his mate."

78

I was trembling. And yes, tears were streaming down my face. I don't know if Goddo was hearing me.

"Do you know what this was?" he said, pressing the head against my cheek.

"I didn't know it was in the box. I promise. I thought it was drugs."

"This was my puppy," he said, and moved away.

His back was to us. We all waited. I don't know how long. He turned to face us again, and I knew I was saved.

"Let him go."

A sort of collective moan came from the gang.

"But what he did . . . Goddo, we've . . ."

"Shut it. Like he said, he's only the messenger. The post boy."

"Still, though, Goddo, we've got him. Yeah, he's the one we've got. Sometimes you have to make do with that. So we send them a message back."

"Least we should do is cut him."

Goddo ignored them. He took another step toward me.

"Come on, Goddo, let's teach them a lesson," said Mickey from the side, his voice quiet, urgent, pleading. "They can't do this. They can't show us this disrespect. This is war."

Goddo looked at him, as if for the first time. And his face changed again. Not angry, not crazy, not laughing. Deadly serious. Suddenly he looked like Roth.

"For once you're right, Mickey," he said. "It *is* war. But this little poof isn't the one." He turned to me. "You said Roth sent this?"

"Roth, yes." I was trembling.

"Tell him something from me. Tell him this. Tell him Goddo's going to kill him. Understand that?"

"Yes."

"You won't forget?"

"No."

"I'm going to help you remember."

And then Goddo opened the jaws of the dog and clamped them around my face, so I had to breathe in the bloody stinking death of it, breathe it down into my lungs. And Goddo scraped the teeth across my cheeks.

TWELVE

"Oh my God."

I hadn't been expecting Maddy Bray to answer the door.

"I'm here to see . . . Shane said to come."

Of course, I should have gone home after the incident with the Temple Moor kids. So why hadn't I? Partly because I wasn't thinking right. I'd spent the time with Goddo and his mates in a state that switched between ordinary fear and absolute terror. And then my life disappeared into the mouth of the dog. And after that I was numb. I was nothing.

But it wasn't just that my head was wrong. There was more to it. It was that I thought Shane could help me. I don't mean with practical things—sorting my face out, dealing with Goddo and Roth, that sort of thing. I mean, I thought he could make me feel better. Stupid, really. I didn't even know him. Didn't know what it was he was supposed to do. But I still thought he could save me, save my soul.

"What happened to you?"

Maddy looked appalled, almost disgusted. I hadn't realized that I was that bad.

"I had some trouble."

"You better come in."

Maddy was still wearing her school uniform, but she'd loosened it up and she looked good.

Shane's house was old and tall. Everything about it, all its points and curves, seemed to reach up to the sky. It made my house, all the houses in my street and the streets around it, feel squat and low and mean, like caves.

Maddy moved to one side and I stepped into the hall. In our house the door opened into the living room. This space echoed like a church, and there were even stained-glass windows, one in the door behind me, another up over the stairs on the landing. The floor was made of little black and white tiles, and for a second I stopped, entranced by them.

"Should I take my shoes off?"

Maddy laughed, and I felt stupid. In our house you always had to take off your shoes when you came in to stop you messing up the carpet.

"I don't think so," she replied, and then I think she felt bad about laughing, because she gave me a nice smile, a sweet smile. "Shane's parents don't seem bothered. Anyway, they're not here. We're all in the basement. Shane'll know what to do. With your face, I mean. Through here."

I followed her down the hall and round into a kitchen full of polished wood and stainless steel, and then through a door and down into a new, dark world. It took me a few seconds to get used to the murk. Then I saw that there were five other kids sitting around on old chairs and a sofa. A big telly was on in the corner.

"Hey, Paul!"

Shane got up and came over to meet me, smiling. When he reached me, his smile disappeared. "What the hell happened to your face?"

The others got up as well now and gathered round. It was oddly like the scene with Goddo and his gang, except with less of a feeling that my throat was about to be slit.

So I told them the whole story. Halfway through, Shane disappeared and came back with a tin box with a red cross on it. He used cotton wool and some stinging stuff out of a bottle to clean the cuts on my face. I was sitting down on the sofa by then, and Shane sat next to me, his face full of concentration and concern.

"Looks worse than it is," he said.

And then I explained how my face came to be like this: the dog, the head, the teeth.

"That's gross," said a girl with white skin and purple

lips. Her lips hadn't been purple when I'd seen her at school earlier that day.

"But its bite was worse than its bark," said another kid, who I didn't know. For some reason I found the remark more annoying than funny.

It was only after I'd finished the story that Shane took the time to introduce the other kids.

"Maddy you know," he said, and then explained to the rest of the gang: "Paul was the one who got her off the hook with Mrs. You Know Who."

"Yeah, I heard about that. Excellent!" said a boy who was really too fat and happy looking to be a freak, but he was going for it anyway.

"This is Billy," said Shane, aiming his thumb at the happy kid, and Billy gave me a wave.

After that I met the purple-lipped girl, whose name was Serena. She didn't seem very interested in me, or anything else for that matter. But you had to say she was pretty, whatever color her lips were. Then there was Stevie, who was eight feet tall and silent. And last of all a boy called Kirk. He was the one who'd said about the dog's bite being worse than its bark.

Kirk looked exactly like Shane. It was uncanny. I don't just mean he wore the same clothes as Shane; he'd somehow made his face look like Shane's face. It wasn't that they had the same features or anything, and when you studied really hard, you could see that they were completely different. But from some power of worship, he'd forced his features into a Shane mask.

"What's your favorite bit?" he said.

I had no idea what he meant. Did he mean my favorite bit of being attacked by the Temple Moor kids?

"*Withnail*, he means," said Billy, the fat one.

"What?" I was still in the dark.

"*Withnail and I*—you know, the movie."

The movie? The film, he meant, on the telly. A DVD.

"Sorry, I've never heard of it."

"Oh, man, it's brilliant," said Billy, already halfway into a rolling laugh. "We've all seen it at least a thousand times. I like Uncle Monty."

"Fatties of the world unite, you have nothing to lose but your chins," said Kirk.

This was all getting really weird. I just didn't understand what anyone was saying.

"Oh, if you haven't seen it you've got a real treat," said Shane. "The first time is always the best, but too often you don't know what it was until it's gone. That's the tragedy of experience."

Then he used the remote to flick the DVD back to the beginning, and for the next hour and a half we all watched *Withnail and I*. It was about two actors in the sixties or maybe seventies, who get drunk all the time and take drugs and do stupid things and it really was quite funny, or it would have been if the freaks hadn't shouted out all the best lines.

But I had a good time. I really did. I needed something to take away the memories of the dog's jaws, and the film did the trick. Billy was friendly, nudging me whenever a really good bit was coming up, and Shane was kind, and Maddy smiled at me twice, which made it three times now, all together. The girl with purple lips—I mean, Serena—didn't say much, and eight-foot-tall Stevie didn't say a word, but that was fine.

The only one I wasn't sure about was Kirk. Everything he said had an edge to it, even if the edge was hidden. An edge of sarcasm, sometimes an edge of something worse. And whenever he spoke, he looked over at Shane to see if he'd heard it, to see if he thought what he'd said was clever. Nothing he said was aimed at me—at least I don't think so, because sometimes it was hard to tell with him. They all knew I'd been through something serious, and it wouldn't have looked good if he'd taken the piss. But I sensed he wanted to. I got the impression that he didn't want an outsider in their group. And, however nice the others were, I was definitely an outsider.

I sensed something else as well. He didn't like the attention Shane paid to me. Didn't like it one bit.

In a quiet part of the film Kirk asked what bands I liked. I'd been dreading something like that. I knew that there were right answers and wrong answers. I sensed the attention of the whole group on me. What were the freak bands? I had a horrible feeling that there were some bands that were fake freak, or freak lite, aimed at nine-year-old girls.

If I picked one of those by mistake, it'd be a disaster. Then I had a flash of inspiration. Go ancient.

"I like the Beatles."

Before Kirk could speak Shane said: "Hey, Paul, good choice. *The White Album* is my second favorite of all time."

"Nice," said Stevie. I think it was the first time he'd opened his mouth.

Kirk looked confused, his eyes darting from Shane to me and back. "Yeah, mine too," he said.

It was fantastically feeble, and even Stevie laughed. Then there was a general discussion, and names flew about, and I lost track of which ones they liked and which were supposed to be lame.

It was nine o'clock when the film finished.

"I'm going to call for a pizza," said Shane. "You want in? We'll put some music on, hang out some more."

"Yeah, give the boy an education," said Kirk, in a way that sounded friendly.

I realized I was hungry, and part of me wanted to stay in this warm dark cave with my new friends. Maybe even find out some more about the music they were raving about. But they weren't really my friends, not yet, and I was worried that I might already have outstayed my welcome, plus my brain was frazzled with all the stuff that had happened today. I needed some time to think, to sort things out in my head.

"No, I'd better be going. My parents . . . Thanks, though."

"OK, that's cool. I'm going upstairs to phone."

I said goodbye to the others. Billy shouted something friendly, and Maddy smiled again. That made four times.

On the way up Shane said, "We didn't really talk much about Roth, about what to do."

"I delivered the package. I did what he said."

"Yeah, I guess you did. But he's . . . dangerous, you know."

I laughed. "Really? I hadn't noticed."

Shane pulled a serious face, and then smiled back. "Sure you have. But I don't just mean that he's a thug, that he can smack you around. I mean he's dangerous . . . God, this sounds stupid . . . dangerous to your soul." I'd never heard Shane sound so uncertain, so unsure of himself. But, strangely, that made me take what he was saying even more seriously. "Do you get me?"

"Yes," I said. "I get you."

"OK then," he said, sounding relieved, but still serious. "So tomorrow, you should hang out with us. When you stick together . . . well, you must have noticed, his sort leave you alone."

"Thanks," I said, a bit embarrassed.

There was music upstairs. Shane opened a door into another huge room, and the sound poured out. It was something classical. I'd never been in a house before where people played music like that. Two adults, Shane's mum and dad, I guessed, were sitting on a funny-looking sofa. They were drinking wine from big, tulip-shaped glasses. They both had their eyes shut. It felt wrong going in there, like walking in on people doing something private.

"Hey, Mum, can I get a pizza for the guys?"

Shane's mother opened her eyes. They were enormous and so blue they looked inhuman, something mineral. There was a kind of stillness to her face. She looked quite a lot like Shane. She was very beautiful.

"Of course, use my credit card when you telephone— it's in my bag in the hall." And then those astonishing eyes turned on me. "Who's your new friend?"

"This is Paul. He got into a bit of a scrape."

Shane's mother stood up and walked over to me. "So I see. And are you going?"

"Yeah, I've got to . . . got to get home."

I blushed. I couldn't meet those blue eyes, and I looked at my feet.

"But you've been hurt." She put out her hand and touched my cheek, where the teeth had cut me.

"It's nothing. It doesn't even hurt. Shane put some stuff on it."

"Well, you must let me give you some money for a taxi."

That made me panic. I'd never been in a taxi. I didn't know how you did it, what you said—I mean, where to go, and how much you gave the driver.

"No, honest, I'm fine, thanks, thank you," I said, and then I basically just ran out of there, shouting a quick good-bye to Shane.

It's raining. Did I say it was raining? No, perhaps I can't say that it is raining. All I can say is that there are huge droplets of rain caught perfectly still in the air. I can see the shape of them, pulled long, like teardrops. I can even see some that have just hit the ground, bursting like tiny bombs. The faces around me are wet. Hair is slicked down and darkened by the rain. And then everything changes. Each drop of rain is suddenly nearer to its explosive little death. And the knife again is closer, the knife shining in the rain.

THIRTEEN

I got in at about ten. My mum and dad were watching the lottery draw on the telly. The living room had layers of stale smoke hanging in it, and Mum was holding a cigarette straight up, balancing a crooked tower of ash. I'd given up nagging at her about smoking. It just annoyed her.

I was supposed to be in by nine. My dad looked round from the sofa.

"Where you been, Paul?" He sounded like he wanted to make the effort to care, but couldn't quite be bothered.

"Just out, Dad. Like I told you, with some friends."

I waited for a couple of seconds to see if he said anything else, or if Mum would say something. But they were lost in the numbers on the telly.

"Is there anything to eat?"

A pause.

They didn't even play the lottery.

"Put yourself some oven chips on," said Mum after the last ball had bobbled into place.

I went to the kitchen and looked in the freezer compartment of the fridge. There weren't any oven chips. There were some peas and a tray of ice. I found some cheese in the fridge, and some white sliced bread in the bread bin, so I made a sandwich. The cheese was hard and cracked, like the skin on an old man's foot. I thought about Shane and the beautiful kitchen in his house, and about his parents listening to classical music with their eyes shut.

Dad came in to put the kettle on. "Cup of tea'll help wash that down," he said, nodding at my stale sandwich.

I should say more about my dad. He's quite tall and broad, and his belly is big and solid, not the kind you can stick your fingers into. But, despite the fact that there was a lot of him, there's something about him that makes you think he's smaller than he is. It might be his head. He's going badly bald, and all his features are squashed into the middle of his face.

My dad's loud. He shouts a lot. And laughs a lot. But his laughing is really a kind of shouting. Even his ordinary talking is loud, as if everyone else is a bit deaf or too far away.

But he's OK, my dad, he really is. Sometimes he collects me from school, either just in the wagon, which was what he called the front bit of the truck, or sometimes the whole thing, with a container hooked on the back. It was worst when the container was for something embarrassing, and it said it on the side. Once the container was full of, you know, ladies' sanitary things, and the next day some kids sang the song from the advert at me. Another time it was for pies, and they all said it was because my dad used to eat a truckload of pies every night. Either way it was pretty embarrassing. He'd honk his horn when he saw me and shout out my name. Sometimes when I saw him waiting out at the front of the school, I'd go back inside and hang around until he'd gone.

Although I hated being collected by him in it, I actually liked it inside the wagon. The seat was worn smooth, and you felt really high up and powerful, and it was where my dad was at his happiest. All the things he used to tell me about when he was at school, and about wars from the past, he told me when he was in his wagon. We didn't talk very much apart from then.

But, like I said, my dad's OK really. He's rough, but he never hits us or anything. He'll sometimes grab me and rub his fist into the top of my head, and that hurts, but he's only playing. I remember when I was little he used to tickle me, but so hard it felt like he was hitting me, and I'd beg him to stop, but he never would. I mean, in my memories he doesn't stop, but just carries on, until I think about something else.

The main thing about my dad is that he's obsessed with war and everything to do with it. All kinds of war. The Greeks and Romans, knights, Trafalgar, Waterloo, Wellington, ships, guns, the Battle of Britain, Lancaster bombers, Stalingrad. He's got loads of war books, as well as a whole shelf of videos we can't play because the machine's bust. He says there's no point getting it fixed because everything just comes out on DVD now. But he won't throw the videos or the machine out, and we don't have a DVD player yet. I read the books too, because they're the only books in the house. Except for Mum's books, which are all about sad ladies falling in love with dark strangers. Actually she doesn't even read those now, because she's too tired.

Mum is the opposite of Dad. She's small and quiet and she looks nice, and she *is* nice when she's not too tired. Although she's the opposite of him, she never disagrees with Dad. Or if she does disagree with him, then it's only in her head and never makes it as far as her mouth. She works really hard. She's a cleaner at the hospital, and she sometimes takes on extra jobs doing offices in town.

But I'm back in the kitchen now, with Dad.

He started looking at me in a funny way. "What happened to your face?" he said suspiciously. "Have you been fighting?"

I don't think he'd have minded that much if I'd said yes. In fact I think he'd have loved it if I had been, and I'd made a joke of it, saying, *You should see the other guy*, or something like that.

"No, Dad. Not really."

"Well, how did you get that on your face then, lad? Did it happen up at Temple Moor?" He sounded more . . . I don't know . . . *disgusted* than concerned. "It looks like a bite or something."

"It's nothing, Dad."

I think I know what he was getting at, what he was worried about. I'm pretty sure my dad was worried that I might be gay, and my face was something to do with that. I really hated him thinking I was gay. It made my insides churn. My dad still thought that there was something dirty about being gay, and that if I was gay then I was dirty. And the thing is, he was so frightened about it that he could never ask me. All he could do was make remarks.

I wasn't hungry anymore, and I didn't want the rest of my sandwich.

"I'm off to bed," I said. I felt sick and angry inside, but also so tired I could hardly get my mouth to work.

"But I've made you some tea. Two sugars."

I thought that maybe I should storm off and slam the door. It was what any decent teenager would have done. But, like I said, my dad wasn't so bad. It was just that he had no idea. It was just that everything had been easy for him. And I was too tired for storming anywhere.

"OK, Dad," I said, my face a mask, "I'll take it up with me."

"Don't spill it on the stairs, son. That carpet's—"

I think he was going to say "new," but then he must have remembered that it was ten years old if it was a day.

FOURTEEN

I'm good at not thinking about things. I feel them rising up in me and then I push them down, the way you do with rubbish in the bin. Some people might say that not thinking about things is a bad idea. But what's the point? What am I supposed to do about someone like Roth, or Goddo, or any of them?

On the way to school I wasn't thinking about anything, except the scrunched Coke can I was kicking. I knew there'd be a gang of kids at the school gates, but I always just walked through them and I hardly ever got bothered. All you have to do is keep looking down, making sure you don't catch an eye.

So I was doing that, my attention on the ground. It's amazing how interesting tarmac can be. Then I felt a hand on my chest.

"Should watch where you're going. Might bump into something. Might do yourself some damage."

Bates.

Then a deeper voice.

"Paul, come here."

Roth.

I looked up. Roth was leaning against the open school gate. Miller cringed and capered beside him. I felt a rush of hatred for him—Miller, I mean; even more than for Roth. I suppose it's because you always hate the one right above you in the order of things, not the one at the top.

"What do you want?" I said, meaning to look Roth in the eye. But it was impossible. My eyes slid off his face like a greasy fried egg sliding off a plate. But still, even if I couldn't meet his black eyes, it wasn't the kind of thing you said to Roth. What you said to Roth was "Yes."

Miller's laugh cut the cold morning air, high and mocking. Except it didn't have the brains in it to mock. Just a noise. Did Roth's blank expression change? I don't know, maybe just a flicker of something. A smile, perhaps, or a sneer, or a grimace.

He beckoned to me and repeated, "Come here." There was no obvious threat in his voice. There didn't have to be.

Without even meaning to, I acted on his words. Before I reached him, Roth sprang forward from the gate. I flinched, expecting a punch or worse. But all I felt was his arm around my shoulders again, heavy as a corpse. He shunted me away from the gates and the mob of kids there, down toward the beck. Miller and Bates followed.

"You deliver my little surprise then?" he whispered, deafeningly, into my ear.

"Yeah."

"To Goddo?"

"Yeah."

"Goddo himself, not one of his mates?"

"Yeah."

Roth waited, his face expectant. I didn't say anything.

"And . . . ?"

"And what?"

Roth had taken his arm from around me. Now he looked me full in the face. For the first time ever there was something juvenile, unsure, about him.

"Listen, Varderman, I've gone easy on you. Stuff you've done, stuff you said, well, it could have got you in trouble. But I always thought you had something. Thought you and me could have been mates. Thought we understood each other. But if you're messing with me . . ."

"You could have got me killed. They had a knife."

My voice cracked when I said "knife." Miller laughed. Roth flicked out sideways with his hand and caught him full in the mouth. Miller went down, holding his face.

"Shut it!" said Roth, not even looking at Miller. "Varderman's right. He did us a job. Went behind enemy lines. More. Went into the den of the beast. And he came back. Gets some respect for that. All right?"

The movement had been minimal, but getting hit by Roth was never a joke, and Miller was on his knees, rocking and weeping silently.

"I said *all right?*"

"Yeah, sorry, sorry."

I stopped hating Miller. For a while.

"Tell me what happened."

"I did what you said. I found Goddo in the sports ground. Gave him the box. He was with his mates. They opened it."

"Yeah? Yeah?"

Roth was so excited he was almost drooling. He was watching me the way a drunk looks at a bottle.

"When they found it . . ."

"What? Go on."

I replayed the scene in my head. Goddo's horror, the near insanity of his reaction. I could have told Roth that, but I didn't want to give him the pleasure.

"He thought it was funny."

"Funny?"

"Yeah. He said he'd been trying to get rid of the dog."

Roth turned to Bates. "You told me he loved that dog. You said he lived for it."

"Yeah, Roth, he did. Everyone knew that. Loved it."

"Doesn't sound like it."

"He didn't seem that bothered to me," I said.

"Well, how come you said you could have been killed then? You said they had a knife."

"Just because Goddo wasn't bothered about his dog doesn't mean he didn't know what you were trying to do."

Roth thought for a while. "You did all right. Thought you'd have run before they got you. Didn't mean them to hurt you." He touched the plaster on my cheek. "What's under there?"

Then I told him what Goddard did with the dog's head. I kept it straight, didn't bother adding anything about the stink of it or anything like that. I think it reached him. I think he felt something. I don't mean sorry about what he'd caused, or sympathy for me. What he felt was that this was an affront to him. They'd put a dead dog's jaws around my face, and that meant they'd done it to him.

"You did all right," he said yet again, nodding.

I felt that something had changed. Somehow I'd come over. I was with him. I mean, that's what *he* thought.

"I've got something for you," he said.

Miller was off the floor by now, and he and Bates were close beside us. Roth reached into his jacket. I felt excited. I didn't want to, but that's how it was.

What was really weird was that this was the only time I'd ever even tried to stand up to Roth—I mean, by telling him the lie about Goddo—and yet I'd somehow found my-self closer to him. It was like the bad dream where there's a monster chasing you, and you feel its breath on your neck, but then suddenly you find that it's standing right in front of you, and rather than running from it you've run *to* it.

"Put your hand out."

I opened my palm.

And then it was there on my hand.

Heavy, solid, slick, perfect.

It was twenty centimeters long. The handle was dark wood, with a polished brass guard where the grip joined the blade. And what a blade. The underside curved smoothly to a drawn-out tip, the line of it leaf-soft, like a living thing. The top of the blade echoed the underside at its tip, but then lost that gentle curving form to become a row of violent sharp teeth. The teeth drew my thumb, and I caressed the line of serrations the way you'd tease and ruffle the fur on a cat's neck.

I knew what they were for. You could catch another blade in those teeth and hold or break it. And if you sank the blade into a soft belly, then the teeth would multiply the harm, turn a cut into a vacant ragged mouth, spewing out its life in a red fountain.

For a few seconds nothing existed in the world except for the knife and me. No, narrower than that. The knife, the hand that held it, the eye that drank in its beauty. Nothing else was left of me.

"Nice, eh?"

I stirred myself. *Nice?*

"Yeah."

"Now, you put that away. You don't talk about it, you don't show it. Understand?"

I nodded.

"Something else." Roth came close to me again, intimate, confiding. His huge face filled the world, the way the moon sometimes seems to take up the whole sky. "Something you'll understand. Not something for these . . . apes here, these baboons. You have this, and there's nothing, no one you ever need to be afraid of. You get it?"

"Yeah, but—"

"That's not all I'm saying. You see, because you're not afraid, you don't need to hate. That's the beautiful thing about it." A smile spread across his face like a tear in the universe. It was one of the most terrible things I'd ever seen, that smile, those small white teeth, each one separate. "And if you don't hate, then you're happy. You get it? Yeah? You with me?" And his eyes were moist, shining with the joy and beauty of what he was saying.

Roth was so close to me now I could feel his breath. I didn't really know what he was talking about, but that was more because I was still living in the knife. But I nodded, longing to get away from him, longing to be alone with the knife. It was only later that I realized that Roth was insane.

"Here, and put it in this," he said, holding out a black leather sheath. "So you don't stab yourself in the nuts."

Harsh laughter from Bates and Miller, the Apes of Roth.

FIFTEEN

That was a strange morning. No one knew about the knife except for Roth and Bates and Miller and me, and yet I felt as though the whole school was treating me differently. Suddenly I had respect. People held doors open for me rather than letting them slam in my face. Nobody barged into me in the corridors or hit the back of my head so my face clanged against the wall above the urinal. When I said things in class, the teacher listened. I even felt taller, as if the figures around me were stooped and cringing.

It was all because of the knife. I could feel its weight in my inside pocket. I kept putting my hand in to caress it. Or I'd deliberately flap my blazer so I could feel its solid mass clunk against my chest, beating against the beating of my heart.

I was still in a dream at morning break. Without thinking about it, I wandered over and joined the freaks in the playground. It was cold and gray, and they were shoulder to shoulder against the world.

"Hey, Paul."

It was Billy, the fat one. His eyes completely disappeared when he smiled.

"Hi, Billy."

I saw that Shane and Maddy Bray weren't there, but Kirk (the Shane-alike, the Shane-lite) and the purple-lipped Serena were, and Stevie the silent one, like a wand of black bamboo.

From his body language I guessed that Kirk had been in the middle of some routine, and he wasn't exactly delighted to see me. He tried carrying on with whatever he'd been saying: ". . . and you can download it for nothing, literally *nothing,* if you go Bit Torrent . . . ," something like that. But he'd lost their interest, assuming he ever had it. So then he said to me, "Saw you talking to Roth earlier on. Thought you'd learned your lesson."

The others looked at me sharply. How could I have gone back to Roth after the horror of the night before?

"Yeah, well, I didn't have much choice."

"Still, you ought to stay away from him. Unless you like getting snogged by a dead dog."

He snorted out a quick laugh at his own joke, but stopped when he saw that the others weren't taking it up.

"He knows that," said Billy, cutting in. Then he added hopefully, "Don't you, Paul?"

I nodded. And then I said, looking at Kirk, "But he doesn't bother you much, does he?"

It was something I'd noticed. True, everyone hated the freaks, but Roth himself never seemed to give them any of his special attention. It was as if they didn't quite register with him. Once or twice I'd seen him gazing in a vague way to where they stood, his eyes unfocused, maybe thinking he ought to do something about them, put in some personal, hands-on persecution, rather than letting the lightweights and no-marks do the job. But then he'd give his head a little shake and move on to some other project.

You could spin that a couple of ways. Either the freaks were so insignificant he didn't have to bother with them, or he felt threatened by their strangeness, worried that maybe his weapons wouldn't work against them. I suppose there was a third option—he just hadn't got around to them yet.

I can't say precisely why, but I knew that saying that, about Roth not bothering them, would get to Kirk. It undermined the freaks' role as victims, made them less like a gang of Jesuses, more like a bunch of nerds.

"We're not exactly best mates, though," he said, his eyes wandering along the horizon, like he was searching for something way off. Trying to look deep.

And just at that moment I saw a ball flying toward us, kicked by one of the mob of Year Eight kids who were playing a cross between football and the Second World War. They'd probably seen it happen the day before and thought how clever it was, belting the ball at the losers. The ball was one of those half-sized ones of silvered leather, and quite heavy. Hurt if they get you in the face. If it had been heading toward Kirk, I'd probably have let it fly on. But it wasn't. It would have hit Serena. And so I caught it. The other freaks had seen it at the last second, and they were all flinching, some throwing their hands up, others cowering down. For some reason the image froze in my head, as if I'd taken a photo of it. They were like a great black spider, legs and arms at crazy angles. Or like the victims of an explosion.

But I caught the ball, and it must have looked quite cool. There was a disappointed sigh from the Year Eights. One of them, not the one who'd kicked it, came up and demanded that I give him his ball back. Yesterday I would have done.

"Nice ball," I said, and began to hand it to him. But then I whipped it away and gave it a massive punt, out over the school fence, over the beck and into the gypsy field beyond, where it bounced a couple of times in the furrows and rucks of the rough grass, and then bobbled out of sight.

The Year Eight kid looked at me, his mouth open. He had close-cropped hair and his ears were scabby and septic from a piercing that had gone tragically wrong.

"What was that for?"

"I felt like it. Next time it's your head."

You could see the confusion in his eyes. These were the freaks, he was thinking, you can kick your ball at them and that'll be funny, and all they'll do is tut at you and then move further away. They don't kick your ball into the gypsy field. They don't talk to you like they're not scared.

And then he trudged off on the long walk out of school, following the road over the beck and round to the gypsy field. It was a good job he was only a scabby Year Eight midget.

"That was awesome," said Billy, in the space after the kid had gone.

"I thought it was a bit mean."

That was Shane. He'd appeared unnoticed in all the action. Maddy was with him.

"But they kicked the ball at us," I said, annoyed that he hadn't appreciated what I'd done. "You always let them, and so they keep on doing it. It's like Hitler."

Everyone laughed at that. I suppose it was a bit of an exaggeration. But that made me want to carry on with it.

"No, I mean it. Like when they didn't stand up to him in the nineteen thirties and so he just carried on getting worse."

"Appeasement," said Kirk, to show he knew the word.

Well, I knew the word as well. It was war. It was my subject.

"So why didn't you thump him then?" said Shane. "You're bigger than him, the kid who wanted his ball back. You should have really taught him a lesson."

It took me a second to realize that he was being sarcastic. Normally when people are being sarcastic you can tell, because they use a special sarcastic voice and even wear a special sarcastic face. But Shane just said it in his normal voice, and his face was his normal face.

It was my turn to be confused now, and I felt just like the Year Eight kid had looked.

"I didn't want to hit him. I just wanted him to . . . I don't know . . . be more careful."

I felt terrible. And I also felt that I shouldn't be feeling terrible. What I'd done wasn't that bad. I'd kicked the ball, not the kid. That made me annoyed with Shane. Who did he think he was to act as my conscience? I began to turn away, my shoulders hunching up around my ears. Then I felt Shane's hand on my arm.

"How's that face of yours?"

And that was it, all trace of criticism was gone, and I was grateful he'd even remembered that I'd been hurt.

Sucker.

I sat at their table for lunch. Serena had brought in a salad made of seeds and bits of weird-shaped lettuce, and Stevie Stick Boy just drank a Coke. But the others had normal food. When I asked Stevie if that was all he was having—the Coke, I mean—he said that he could only eat when it was dark. And then Kirk said it was because he was a vampire, and Shane said not to be a dick because vampires didn't drink Coke and anyway it was the middle of the day right now, so if Stevie was a vampire he'd be burning, wouldn't he? Then they got on to talking about vampires in general, which was a big thing with them. Shane said it was funny how vampires, meaning Dracula in particular, came to be seen as aristocrats, counts and stuff, because originally they'd just been shambling peasants, and he said it was all down to Byron, or rather his doctor, whose name I can't remember, who wrote a story about a posh vampire, which was really meant to be Byron. I was a bit lost in all this, and I think Shane knew it, because then he explained that two hundred years ago Byron was not only the most famous poet, but the most famous human being in England, and that he had a clubfoot and he got off with everyone, including choirboys and his own sister. And his wife divorced him because he tried to do something to her so filthy that she could never even talk about it. So it meant that his doctor's story—the one about the vampire—became really famous really quickly, and that's how the idea of the posh vampire took hold.

I thought that was all quite interesting, even if none of them could tell me exactly what a clubfoot was, which is something I wanted to know. What was strange is how it didn't seem strange, all that talk. It wasn't as if I normally spent my meal times talking about vampires and dead poets, and so it should have freaked me out. But it didn't.

The other thing was that I forgot about the knife.

Then, at the end, I was stretching to get my bag from under the table, and I touched Maddy's hand by accident. I said sorry, and she smiled at me again. Number five. Then I stretched further, trying to reach my bag, and something fell out of my blazer pocket. Like I said, I'd completely forgotten about the knife, and it took me a second to realize what had happened. It clunked on the tiles, still in its leather sheath. Maddy picked it up for me, not thinking.

And then she saw properly what it was, and she held it out on her palm, her eyes wide.

"What the hell . . . ?" said Kirk.

I snatched the knife and looked around at my new friends. They all appeared stunned. And something else. Impressed, maybe? Amused, slightly? I don't know.

Except Shane. He looked utterly blank. I couldn't face him.

"I've got to go," I said, to no one in particular, and then I bolted.

Although my eyes are on the knife and the hand that holds the knife, I become aware of something behind me. A shadow. A presence. But it is soft and blunt and it cannot hurt me. So I dismiss it. Everything must reach forward, all my mind must be focused on the knife, on the boy.

SIXTEEN

A few days later I saw it happen.

Those days had been good. I'd been hanging out with Shane and his gang. For the first time since going to that school I felt like part of something. I wasn't really a full member of their gang, and I hadn't turned freak, not really. But I had changed. I looked a bit different, and I was thinking about things I hadn't thought about before. About the world and what was wrong with it—not just the tiny bit of it that I was in, but the whole world. When I walked, I didn't always keep my head down. I hadn't got up the courage to talk to Maddy much, but she didn't seem to mind if I stood near her in the playground or sat next to her at lunch.

It wasn't all good. Kirk didn't like me, and quite often he'd make sure the talk went in a direction I couldn't follow. But Kirk was only one kid. And I knew from experience that getting snubbed was a hell of a lot better than getting punched.

Anyway, the next Wednesday afternoon I was in the science lab on the third floor. The sinks there overlook the back of the school. Out that way you first have a small square of playground, then the big rectangle of the all-weather field, then the fence and the school gates, and then a building that used to be a social club but is now a nothing, a shell like a rotten tooth. There's always graffiti on the walls of the club. Body parts, names, swearwords—all that. I once thought that I should do it too—make my mark on the wall, I mean. I bought a can of white spray paint and sneaked out late. But then, when I reached the club and stood in front of the wall, I couldn't think of anything to write. I shook the can so it made that rattling noise, but nothing else. I didn't have a nickname I could spray, and there wasn't a girl I fancied, not then. I didn't want to write the name of a crappy football team, and I didn't want to copy the other things scrawled there, the f-words and the c-words and the ugly pictures. I was as empty as the social club. So I threw the can into the gypsy field and went home again.

But now, looking out over the back of the school, I saw that some kid was doing what I hadn't been able to do. I couldn't make out what he was spraying, but there was no mistaking that combination of sweeping arm movements and quick little steps.

Words.

I watched him for as long as it took me to wash out my test tube, not thinking much about who he was or what he was writing. I didn't even point it out to the kids on either side of me.

I'd forgotten about it by going-home time. But then I saw the crowd. I remember in junior school, we had some tadpoles. Someone had found a jellied mass of spawn in the beck, which was a miracle, because nothing was supposed to live in there except rats and thick green scummy weed. We fed them with a little piece of meat tied to some string. It took the tadpoles a while to realize that it was dinnertime, but then they'd all swim over to the meat. What happened then wasn't really what you'd expect. They wouldn't go mad, like sharks having a feeding frenzy. No, they'd all gather round the meat, shoulder to shoulder, nudging closer but hardly moving. Sometimes one would wriggle for a few seconds, but then go back to the patient nudging and crowding. You couldn't really see them eat because their mouths were too small.

The kids gathered around the wall were like that, all pressing forward, some wriggling, but mainly just this concentrated, passive attention.

I was with a kid called Emmery. He wasn't really a friend of mine, but we sometimes walked home together because he lived in the same street. Emmery was a bit gorm-less, but all right apart from that. He had to get another kid to do his tie after PE, and he wore slip-on shoes to get around the problem of laces.

"Something going on," he said.

"Looks like it. I think I saw someone spraying on the wall earlier."

"A kid?"

"Yeah, but not one of ours, I don't think."

"Was it another thingy?"

Emmery laughed, a moist, slightly mental laugh. He was talking about last year, when a really big dirty picture appeared on the wall. It was famous for a while.

"Dunno."

We joined the back of the crowd.

"What does it say?"

Emmery could read, just, but the writing was too scraggy for him.

It was about Roth.

It was really bad.

It said things about him—about what he liked to do, about what he liked having done to him. I wanted to laugh. I wasn't the only one. The crowd of kids thrummed with a sort of suppressed glee. But no one was going to show it, not with Roth himself standing there in front of the wall.

He was looking at the writing. I could see half of his face, and his jaw was clamping and loosening, clamping and loosening. Other than that it showed nothing. Miller and Bates were with him. They looked nervous, glancing from Roth to the wall to the kids in the crowd. I had no idea how it was going to end. In a way I didn't want it to. It was the best thing that had happened since I came to this crappy school.

Then a little kid pushed to the front of the crowd, elbowing his way through and raising a protesting cloud of tuts around him. It was the same squirt who'd come to get the ball from me that day. He read the writing on the wall to himself, his lips moving silently. Then he began to smirk. Then smile. Then his whole face lit up into a huge grin. And finally the laughter poured out of him in a frothing, bubbling waterfall.

Either he hadn't seen Roth, or he didn't know who he was. Roth didn't bother much with the younger kids, same as he didn't bother with the freaks, so it was possible the kid just didn't make a connection between the name on the wall and the brooding monster next to him.

Big mistake.

The next thing that happened was pretty obvious. That first laugh was enough to set the whole crowd off. Someone spluttered, then in a great rush we were all laughing and screaming like a load of baboons. It was a real moment of freedom and release. I don't know how well I've got across to you how our school wasn't a happy place. It was a place where you always felt like there was a belt around your chest, tightening, squeezing, and another weight on your head, keeping you bowed down, eyes to the ground. But in a second those two weights—the one around the chest, the one on the head—were gone, and our souls soared up on those clouds of laughter. I was laughing so hard that tears were streaming from my eyes. I know it's one of those things you say, *I laughed till I cried,* but I really did, wiping away the tears with the rolled-back cuffs of my jumper. And for once we were united together, and it felt good and strong, and Roth seemed smaller compared to us, no longer a creature out of our nightmares, but just a bully and, like all bullies, helpless when his victims stood together.

It couldn't last.

Roth was slow to act, but when he moved, he was like a predatory beast. He spun and grabbed the kid, lifted him up. Had one hand on his throat, the other on the scruff of his neck. So the kid was choked at the front, yanked at the back. His laughter stopped, and his face took on a look of bemusement, followed by the agony of the grip, and then, as the reality of his situation dawned, the terror of what would follow. And our laughter stopped too, as if we'd been turned off with a switch, and we were no longer together, but alone.

"Funny, eh? Yeah, funny."

Roth spoke quietly, but everyone could hear him. The kid made a gurgling sound. It was the sound that comes with death in bad films.

"Trouble is, it's a bit of a mess. Doesn't look good. Ought to clean it up, really. Give us a hand, eh? Yeah?"

Then he did something grotesque—I mean, even by his standards. He made the kid's head nod, the way you sometimes see children make their dolls or teddies nod when they talk to them. The kid's face was rigid and waxy with horror.

"Good boy. That's it."

And then Roth lifted up the face of the kid and put it to the rough brick of the wall.

"Let's give it a clean, yeah, eh?"

The kid made a wailing sound, maybe the most horrible thing I've ever heard. His legs, like the legs of a hanged man, began to thrash in the air. I wanted to do something, but like the rest of the crowd I was paralyzed by the evil before us. Not just the fear of it, but the spectacle itself. Evil as a circus.

"That won't work."

Shane.

Doing his trick of appearing from nowhere.

Roth, still holding the kid, slowly turned his black gaze on Shane. "What?"

How much hatred can you get into an innocent word? No, not hatred. Some place beyond hatred, because hatred can burn off or burn out or lose itself in the passage of time. This was something ancient, immortal. This was the mouth that comes up from the deep to eat you, the mouth that has been eating you for a hundred million years, the mouth that will never stop eating you.

"It'll still be there. Worse than that. All you'll do is draw attention to it. People will point to it, say that's where you mashed that kid into the wall."

The voice was cool, light; serious, but amused. Each word formed and perfect. I wished it was my voice. My voice slurred and stumbled and got muddled. Shane's words were like pebbles he'd found on the beach, beautiful and shiny, and all he had to do was hold them out in his hand.

Then there was a movement and Shane lurched forward, slapping against the wall. It was Bates. He'd flung himself into Shane's back. Miller made his whooping laugh, but it lacked mirth, lacked conviction. Everything about it was crap—the cowardice, the timing.

"Yeah, very brave," said Shane, a little smile on his face. I noticed then that there was something in his hand. "Doesn't help *you* much, though, does it?" he said to Roth.

Roth stared back at him, the kid still hanging like a rabbit in his hands.

"But me, I can fix it."

"What?"

That was a different "what." Puzzled now, interested.

"Shall I?" said Shane, holding up what was in his hand.

It was a spray-paint can.

Roth grunted.

Then Shane stepped up to the wall, to the writing. The letters were crude and spaced.

He sprayed.

Roth grunted again.

Someone in the crowd laughed. A new laugh, this one. Not the release of hysteria we'd heard before. This was a laugh of satisfaction, of us against them. And the them was the teachers. The laughter became general.

Shane had done something simple. He had turned Roth into Rothman. Rothman taught history. Nobody cared much about Mr. Rothman. His voice was high and quavery, and he threatened a lot, but he never delivered. If you had to put a word to what most people thought about Rothman, you'd probably hit on "contempt." And now his name was up there instead of Roth's. It was Mr. Rothman, school-teacher, who was said to do those things, to like having those things done to him.

And Shane had done a good job. The scrawl exactly matched the original. It didn't matter that we all knew it was meant to be Roth. It now said Rothman, so Rothman was what it meant.

Roth dropped the kid. He scuttled away on all fours, too frightened to stand up straight. All the time Roth's eyes never left Shane. Now he nodded. Shane met his eyes. He nodded back.

People drifted away, reluctantly at first, worried in case they should miss something, but soon there was just Shane and me and the kid, who was squatting on his haunches against the wall. I don't know where the rest of the freak gang were.

"You OK?" Shane took the kid by the hand, pulled him up gently. "What's your name?"

"Skinner."

"I don't mean your surname. What's your first name?"

"Kevin."

"Well, Kevin, you're a lucky kid."

The boy looked up at Shane. His eyes were glistening. His lips formed words, but I didn't hear, and I don't know if it was some kind of thanks or a mumbled curse, because sometimes you hate the people who help you. Either way, the kid was up and running and lost in the streets of red-brick houses.

SEVENTEEN

Afterward Shane looked dead, like some creature washed up on the shore.

"You want to come back to mine?" he said, his voice sounding like it was coming from another room in a big house.

And the two of us walked there, hardly speaking, but our shoulders touched and our feet were in step. At the end of his road Shane stopped, and I stopped with him.

"That knife . . ."

No one had mentioned the knife since I'd dropped it.

I'd thought of all kinds of excuses, all sorts of reasons. But I wasn't going to lie now.

"Roth . . . he made me take it."

"You know, you can't hang out with us if you've got a knife. It's just not cool."

"I know. I didn't want it. I'll chuck it."

That was it. That was all. I needed someone to tell me what to do, and Shane had.

At his house we went straight down to the basement. Stevie was there. I was disappointed for a moment.

"Hey," he said. Then, "What's up?"

I looked at Shane, thinking he would tell the story. But he just sat down, saying nothing. So I told it. The words poured out of me. I've never been a good talker, but now it was as if I'd been waiting all my life for this. I told about the graffiti, and the crowd, and Roth champing away like he was eating souls, and the kid and the laughter, and the horror of Roth treating him first like a puppet and then like a dish rag, and about Shane saving his life. I know that was an exaggeration, but it seemed right. I imagined the kid's head worn to a bloody stump after scouring the brick.

All the way through Shane looked down at his trainers, moving his head sometimes, as if he was going to disagree with something, but he never said a word. At the end there was silence. I was worn out with the telling, and Stevie was stunned.

"You want to play a game or something?" Shane said

into the void, meaning his Xbox. We shook our heads. Another pause.

"Spliff?"

Stevie nodded. "Yeah, maybe—if there was ever a time, I mean, it's now."

I felt a little surge of excitement. I'd never taken anything. Mainly because of that kid who died after he sniffed a can of lighter fluid. I know it's not the same, but it sort of put me off.

Shane reached under the old settee and came out with a tin. The tin had two cigarettes in it, a packet of rolling papers and a plastic wrap of brown resin.

Shane looked at me. Maybe my face was letting on that this was new, that this was something I didn't know how to deal with.

"It's not skunk or anything," he said.

"Doesn't your mum . . . you know?"

"She's OK. As long as it's just this."

He rolled the joint as he spoke, breaking up one of the cigarettes for the tobacco. His fingers trembled slightly.

"Want me to do it?" said Stevie, looming over, tall even when he was sitting down.

"What?" Shane's voice was sharp and aggressive. Not Shane's voice at all.

"Just thought . . ."

"Well, don't think."

Stevie looked down. His face was red.

Shane finished the joint, lit it with a disposable lighter, inhaled deeply and sank back into the settee. Three big hits later he passed it to Stevie, along with a look that said sorry for the harsh words. He could do a lot with a look.

The smell from the joint was heavy and sweet and sickly, and I felt a quick spasm of nausea. Stevie took a couple of drags and held it out to me. I hesitated for a moment. I didn't want to smoke the joint, but I wanted to be part of it, part of them.

"Have you not . . . ?" said Stevie, sensing my reluctance. "It's cool, you know. I don't mean doing it, I mean *not* doing it. Don't do stuff you don't want to do. That's the rule."

That was the longest speech I'd heard him make. If he'd pushed it harder, I'd probably have pushed back. But now he'd made it seem like I had a choice, which meant I had to give it a go. I took the joint. I'd never even smoked a cigarette, so I had no idea what to do with my breath. I sucked, and the sticky smoke filled my mouth. It didn't get any further. I exploded into a cough, my eyes watering, my head spinning.

And that did it.

Suddenly all the tension in the room—the pent-up fear and adrenaline—evaporated, and the three of us began to laugh, and the laughter took us literally onto the floor, rolling and choking and coughing and spluttering.

When we'd stopped, Shane relit the joint and he and Stevie smoked it down. I had a couple more drags, and managed not to cough. Not much, but enough, I guess.

"That was the bravest thing I've ever seen," I said, in a quiet moment. "When he looked at you, I thought he was gonna kill you. That kid is a freak of nature."

And that set us off laughing again, and we didn't really stop for an hour, and then I said it was time for me to get home.

"Me too," said Stevie, and we left together. As I was leaving, Shane put his hand on my arm.

"What we talked about . . . you said you'd get rid of it?"

"I will. I don't want it."

"OK."

At the front door I realized I'd forgotten my bag. I went back down to the basement. I opened the heavy door quietly. The settee faced away from the door, and I had a mind to give Shane a shock, yelling out—you know how you do.

There was something funny about the way Shane was sitting. He was smoking the other cigarette from the tin. Not a joint, just as a cigarette. His arm was stretched out, white in the gloom.

He took the cigarette out of his mouth.

I could see the end glowing.

And then he put the cigarette to his arm, the underside of his arm, and stroked it down from his elbow to the blue veins of his wrist. It was a gentle movement, tender, as if he was playing with a child or a cat or a girl. And then he lifted the cigarette to his mouth again and drew on it, and then quickly stubbed it down into his arm, not gentle now, not gentle at all. His body went tense for a moment, and then

softened, and he fell back onto the settee and let the cigarette roll down onto the carpet.

I backed out of the door and ran up the stairs. Stevie
was gone, and I went out into the cold night, running, and
then I put my hand on a low brick wall, and first retched,
and then spewed and spewed and spewed.

On the way home I thought about chucking the knife
in the beck. I took it out of its sheath. Looked at the blade
glinting in the streetlights. Felt its lovely weight, its balance,
its calmness. I thought about Shane hurting himself. I'll put
it away somewhere safe, I thought.

Perhaps this battlefield is like a chess game. I don't mean that there is a strategy here. There is no strategy. There is only horror and confusion. I mean that in between the moves, all is utterly static. Walk away and the game would remain as it is for eternity. Or at least until the board and the pieces crumble to dust.

EIGHTEEN

The next morning everyone was buzzing about it, how there was going to be a fight, how we were going to get our revenge. The Templars had trespassed on our territory, written stuff on our wall, showed us no respect. I didn't hear any talk about the dog's head, about how Roth had begun this. In fact I didn't hear any sense at all. Some kids said that the fight was going to be up there. Some said down here. Everyone knew it was going to be dirty. The talk was that Roth was going to cut Goddo. There were even different versions of this, depending on who you spoke to. Some said he was going to cut him open. Cut him so he wouldn't be alive anymore. Some just said cut, like it was a lesson. I don't know if any of this went back all the way to Roth, or if it was something people guessed was going to happen, based on Roth's reputation.

At morning break I went and stood with the freaks. By now it was natural. It was what I did. Stevie was telling them about the wall and about the kid and about Shane, using my words. I didn't mind. I was pleased, in fact. They were good words. Kirk was loud in his praises of Shane's courage, and that was only right. Then he turned to me.

"And you were there?"

He sounded bright, friendly.

That should have been a warning.

"Yeah," I said modestly, thinking that being there was a good thing, that I had the special status of a firsthand witness, a primary source.

"That was lucky, for Shane."

I still wasn't really thinking, and I said, "Yeah," again, missing the first quick, sharp sting of sarcasm.

"Having you there to back him up."

Then I began to get it.

"Having you on his side."

Now I was staring Kirk in the eye.

"And you did *what*, exactly? Just so we can get it straight."

"Hang on—" said Billy, the fat one.

"No, really, I'm intrigued," said Kirk, over him. "So,

Paul, while Shane was rescuing this little kid, you were . . . what, *exactly?*"

"It wasn't like that . . . it was—"

Then I saw Maddy. She was watching me. She looked pretty today. She still hadn't got the freak thing right, but she'd hit on a nice look, for her. Her hair was tied back. And her neck . . . I don't know. Something about her neck. I want to say it was like a swan, but that isn't right. I only want to say it because that's what you say about a neck when you think it might be beautiful. You say swanlike. But a human with a neck like a swan would be a monster. I think what I liked about Maddy's neck was that the curve of it seemed made to have a cheek rest into it. And my mind was already there, resting into her neck, my skin on her skin.

"You didn't help him?"

Maddy. A sting.

"Yes . . . no . . . there were kids everywhere . . . I couldn't . . ."

"Without Paul they'd have kicked the shit out of me."

Shane. Not there and then there. And his words bit, because he didn't usually swear.

Kirk turned to him, his face uncertain, his eyes shifting, troubled, but reluctant to let this one go.

"That's not what Stevie said. Stevie said he just stood there, like a dummy."

I felt the freak crowd draw in its breath.

"I never said dummy."

"That's what you meant," said Kirk, a little more sure of himself now. "That's what it amounted to."

"Stevie," said Shane, "who told you about it? About what happened?"

Stevie looked puzzled for a moment, then smiled. "Paul. I just repeated what he told me."

"And when have you ever heard him boast about anything?" Shane began by looking at Stevie, but then shifted his gaze to Kirk, and then to the gang in general.

"He never talks about himself," said Billy, grinning. "He's a modest guy."

"I'm telling you all now, without Paul watching my back, I'd have been in trouble."

Maddy gave me a little smile. I could have kissed Shane. Or Maddy. Or both. It was like a dream. I was getting praised at the same time for being brave *and* for being modest.

Kirk didn't want to leave things there, with him looking stupid and me looking good, so he changed the subject.

"You all know there's going to be a big fight, don't you?"

Yeah, we knew.

"Have you heard the latest?"

"Do tell," said Stevie, deadpan.

"It's tomorrow. They're coming down here to the gypsy field."

"You sound like you're looking forward to it," said Shane.

"What if I am? All it means is that two sets of meat-heads are going to beat each other to a pulp. What's not to like?"

"What if someone gets hurt?" I asked.

"Like I said, if they're all idiots, who cares?"

"What if someone gets *badly* hurt? What if someone gets put in hospital?"

Kirk laughed. I think some of the others laughed with him. I could see that I was coming across as a bit straitlaced. I should have learned by now that in an argument at school it's always the one who is most serious who loses.

"Read my lips," said Kirk. "I don't care. *Their* psychos or *our* psychos, doesn't matter."

"What if someone gets killed?"

"Hospital or morgue, I couldn't give a toss. One less nutter."

Just before break was over the group split up, each person set on some individual project. I found that I was standing alone with Maddy.

It was what I wanted.

What I dreaded.

The truth is that I'd never really spoken to a girl before. I mean, apart from hair-pulling and name-calling when I was little. My mind went blank. No, not blank. It was full of stuff, words and ideas whizzing round. But I couldn't get my hands on any of them, so the effect was the same.

Silence.

Maddy saved me.

"Dirk's a kick," she said. Then there was a little pause while it sank in.

Then we laughed. Loud with the release. Too loud, perhaps.

"Kirk's a dick, I meant."

"Yeah," I said, still smiling. "Why do you lot put up with him?"

"We're not like that. They don't exclude anyone."

It was funny how she went from "we" to "they." Decoding it was easy. Look at you and me, she was saying. If there was any excluding going on, don't you think we'd be at the top of the list?

"Shane's amazing, though, isn't he," I said, following some weird connection of my own.

Maddy's face lit up. "Yeah. And you were there. There when he saved that kid. I'm glad it was you. I don't think any of the others would have been brave enough to back him up. Not Kirk, anyway. Stevie would have tried, but, you know . . ."

"Yeah, he looks like he'd break in two if you blew on him."

Maddy giggled.

I went for it, surfing on the energy wave.

"So, well, do you want to maybe hang out sometime?"

"We hang out all the time."

Her face, her tone, were hard to read. Friendly, half smiling. But was she saying no, or was she teasing, asking for more? If she hadn't said the nice things about me, about being brave, I'd have given up. But I *was* brave: I'd been the one to stand by Shane in his hour of need.

"No, I mean, would you like to go to see a film or something? You know, you and me. Together."

God, but that was lame.

Then I noticed that Maddy's eyes had drifted beyond me. I looked round. Shane was waiting near the school entrance.

"Oh heck," she said. "Look, Shane's waiting. We're going to be late for chemistry."

"Tonight?" I said quickly, clutching at air, hoping, doubting.

"Tonight? Yes, OK, fine."

She said yes. She definitely said yes. Wings. Flying.

"Let's meet at the multiplex. At eight. We can see anything—anything you like."

"Anything, yes."

Maddy was itching to get to the lesson. That was OK. She was a geek.

And then, her face filling with a smile, she ran toward him—Shane, I mean, and chemistry.

NINETEEN

I was walking into the building when a hand grabbed the arm of my blazer, pinching my flesh. I let out a quick scream, which was stupid. One of the first things you learn is to hide your pain, because pain is what they love, and it works like a blood trail in the water. But it was the surprise, not really the pain, and how can you guard against being surprised? Anyway, it was answered by the hyena laughs of Miller and Bates. Roth loomed behind them, his black eyes glittering in the shadows.

Bates, who'd grabbed me, pushed me toward his master,

at the same time wrenching and twisting at the soft under-flesh of my arm.

"Paul, Paul," said Roth, his voice soft and deep, pretending hurt, "you've been avoiding me." He stepped forward, opening his arms like a priest. "I thought we were mates. I thought we were going to spend some time together. I thought we'd be down the park, throwing a Frisbee to each other, swapping jokes, having a laugh."

And I almost did laugh at the thought of Roth with a Frisbee. It was like imagining Genghis Khan with a yo-yo.

"He's got his new friends now," said Miller, giggling. "He's all over them freaks. He must fancy one of them."

"Which one, do you reckon?" said Bates, joining in. "The lanky one? Or wassisname, the chief bummer?"

"Shut up."

That made them all laugh, even Roth, who usually saved it for leap years.

"Ooooooo," said Miller, "look at her. I think we got it."

"Nah, look, let's not get nasty," Roth said, putting his arm around me in that way of his, heavy and threatening. "This is a time we all have to stick together. You know why, don't you."

"The fight."

"The fight," he says. "The fight. You make it sound like two Year Seven bitches having a bit of a scratch behind the bike sheds. This isn't a fight, this is war. It's us against them. And do you know who they are, eh?"

I nodded, meaning the Temple Moor kids, the evil kids who didn't go to our school, kids who lived just up the road.

"Barbarians. That's it. You're a clever kid, aren't you, eh, yeah? You've listened in history. You know about the Spartans, don't you?" Roth's eyes weren't on me now, but were focused somewhere else, thousands of years ago, many many miles away. "You know about how they stood together, shield to shield, while the Persians splashed against them like waves on a rock?"

That was the thing about Roth. He could say things like that, things you'd never think were in him. Maybe if things had been different for him, if he'd been brought up somewhere else, with a different mum and dad, he'd have achieved something, done something amazing.

"That's us. Spartans. The Templars are the barbarians. The way white men beat barbarians is by sticking together, keeping that shield wall tight. You get me?"

I nodded. There wasn't much else I could do. But I also looked quickly at Miller, a black kid, not a white man. And I thought I saw something there, something beneath that cowed, craven look of his.

Roth caught my glance, but he couldn't have seen Miller's expression.

"You don't worry about him," he said, and I wasn't sure who he was speaking to. Maybe it was himself. "Miller's all right. Miller's one of us. We've civilized you, eh, yeah?"

And Miller didn't say anything for a moment, and then he grunted, which I suppose meant yes.

And then Roth focused on me again.

"You've still got it, yeah?"

Of course I knew what he meant.

"Yes."

"Got it here?"

I shook my head. It was in my secret hiding place.

"Sensible. I knew you had brains. Some thick kid would have carried it around like a mobile. Not you. Feels good, though, doesn't it? Having it, touching it."

I thought about the knife, felt it invisible in my hand.

"It feels . . . good, yes."

Bates made a hissing noise. A sigh, I think.

"Tomorrow. You'll bring it tomorrow?"

I wanted to say no; to say that I didn't want anything to do with the stupid fight. The best I could manage was to say nothing.

"Reckon he's chicken," said Bates.

"Nah, not my mate Paul. He's a good lad."

Roth squeezed me again with his big arm.

"And when he hears what they were saying, well, then he'll be up for it, won't you, eh?"

I didn't get it for a second.

"Who do you mean? What did they say?"

"It's all right, we know there's nothing in it. We know they're a bunch of lying savages, monkeys, apes, don't we, eh?"

"What did they say?"

"Forget it."

"Tell me."

"They said you liked it when they made you kiss the dog. They said it was the kind of thing you liked. They said stuff like that."

And then he told me some other things. The kind of things that had been written on the wall, about him.

"Now, the point is," he said, his voice low and reasonable, like we were talking about what was on the telly tonight, "that kind of thing gets around. When it gets around, it becomes true. As good as true, I mean. I'm saying that no one can tell the difference between the lie and the truth. And when you can't tell the difference between a lie and the truth, then, you know what, there isn't a difference. Because the truth is only what people think it is. So what you need to do is put any thoughts like that out of people's heads. You get stuck in tomorrow, and what are people gonna say then? Not that you're the dog snogger. No, they're gonna say you're a hero. They'll remember you for a long time."

I felt sick. I didn't believe that lies and the truth were the same—the same underneath, I mean. But Roth was right in that the truth sometimes can't protect you against the lie; that the lie is sometimes stronger than the truth.

But feeling sick isn't the same as wanting to fight.

"I don't care what people say about me."

Roth's face changed slowly. He'd been working it up to now, making the muscles move into the human shapes that other faces had. But now it was slack and empty, and I knew that I was in terrible trouble.

"He doesn't care what people say about him," he said, his voice like the voice of a dead man, a spirit, calling from beyond the tomb.

And then action.

I was against the wall, my face crushed in his hands.

"But what about his dad, eh? Yeah, his dad." I could feel his breath on my face, but it had no odor, nothing, nothing at all. "I've heard how he was always going on about what a tough guy he was at school. Oh yeah. How he was the hero at the big fight up at Temple Moor all them years ago. Well, you know what? I heard different. I heard that he shat himself. I heard he was a coward. You a coward too, eh, Varderman? Another good story to put around, that one, eh? Your dad, shitting himself."

And I fought against the hand on my face and the weight of Roth pushing me against the wall, fought as hard as I could, but I was like some soft creature writhing under the tracks of a tank. And Roth laughed.

"That's a bit more like it," he said. "A bit of fight in you, eh? That's good, really good. Doesn't matter so much if your dad was chickenshit. You can put that right. You can be the one with guts in your family. That's it, eh, yeah?"

And then he put his hand inside my blazer and began to feel me, and then he moved his hand down to my trousers, and then up again, and then he said, "You sure you haven't got it, my little girl, my baby?"

"I told you, no, it's not here," I said, squirming under his grip.

"Yeah, well, that's good, good. But I told you what a friend that knife could be to you. And you haven't got many, have you?"

"He's got them weirdos," said Bates.

"They're not really your friends, you know, Paul. They don't care about you. You're not one of them. When push comes to shove, they won't watch your back. They'll leave you in the shit."

I should have defended them, but it was easier to say nothing.

"But tomorrow, you'll bring it?"

"The knife."

"Yeah, the knife. Bring it. Use it. Make everything right."

I nodded my head. But in my heart I said no.

TWENTY

I opened the door. The telly was on in the living room, but there was nobody there. I once asked my mum why she left the telly on all the time, even when she was out. She said she liked it, that it felt friendly. I turned it off.

I went up to my room. I hadn't spoken to anyone for the rest of the day. At lunch I went to the library and sat in a corner and opened a book. I don't know what the book was about. I didn't try to read it. For a while I thought about what Roth had said. About the Temple Moor kids saying bad things about me. About my dad being a coward, and not brave at all. About him being a liar. To say that I thought about it gets it wrong. I didn't think about it: it was just there in my head like a cancer or something. Yeah, a brain tumor. And it's not as if you can do anything about a brain tumor by thinking about it. *Hey, brain tumor, I've decided you're a bad idea, so why don't you go away now? Oh, OK, if you say so. Bye then. Yeah, bye.*

I looked around my room. Ever since I'd got to know Shane and his gang I'd begun to feel funny about lots of things in my life. I mean, funny in a bad way. Feel that they weren't right, weren't good. My clothes, my hair, my things. There was nothing good about my room. The walls were plain. I don't even know what you'd call the color. It wasn't gray, but it was grayish, and with something a bit yellow in the gray, and maybe something a bit pink. The curtains were blue with lines on. The lines were black. There was a chest of drawers that was older than me, but not old enough to be interesting. There was a wardrobe with a tall mirror on the inside of the door. So you had to open the door to look at yourself. That was stupid.

I opened the door and looked at myself. I didn't like what I saw. I wasn't ugly. I wasn't good-looking. I was nothing. My hair was like the walls—no real color. There was still something unformed and babyish about my face. I squeezed it with my hands, the way Roth had squeezed it. Wanting to hurt myself, wanting to squeeze out the thoughts.

And then I remembered, and the thoughts of Roth and my dad, the coward, shitting himself when he should have been fighting, were blown away like leaves in an autumn gale.

Maddy.

I was going to the cinema with Maddy.

And suddenly I was happy and excited, and looking back at myself in the mirror, I thought that maybe I didn't look too bad.

I changed out of my school clothes. I had some OK jeans—nothing special, nothing great, but not embarrassing. And I had an OK shirt. It was actually an old one of my dad's. It was a creamy color, and the thick cotton was smooth with age, and it only had buttons down to the middle, so you had to put it on over your head. I suppose it was kind of old-fashioned, but I thought it looked timeless. Jeans and a shirt and trainers. The trainers were OK too, just a pair of standard black and white Adidas. You wouldn't notice them either way, to love or to hate.

I brushed my teeth and washed my face. I got some water on the front of the shirt and some toothpaste on my jeans, and I felt stupid for not getting washed before I got dressed. But my mind was all full up with the excitement and the fear of seeing Maddy.

And when I was washing, I decided that I wasn't going to go to the fight tomorrow, wasn't going to have anything to do with Roth and his thugs. Let them fight. I didn't care what the Temple Moor kids had said. And I didn't know what my dad had done all those years ago, and didn't much care about that either. None of it mattered, not compared to seeing Maddy.

I heard voices and smelled food. I hadn't noticed my parents come in. I went downstairs.

"Got fish and chips," said my dad.

I didn't want to meet Maddy stinking of chip fat. Anyway, I wasn't hungry.

"I'm off out."

"Have something first," said Mum. She was smoking as she unwrapped the fish from the paper, glistening translucent with the fat.

Dad was sitting at the kitchen table. He had already started to eat his chips, picking some off the paper as he rolled the rest onto his plate.

"Dad?"

"Yes, son?" he said, not looking up. The bald top of his head was pointing at me. It also glistened, as if he'd rubbed it in the chip paper.

I was glad that Maddy and the others weren't here to see this. Because there was another thing that they had taught me: to be ashamed of my parents, and our house, and the way we lived. And, still looking at the strangely soft, vulnerable, glistening head of my dad, the skin pink and blotched with brown freckles, the shame I'd felt was replaced, slowly, by guilt. My mum and dad had worked hard all their lives. When they weren't working, they were tired, and what they liked to do was sit and watch the telly eating fish and chips. It wasn't a crime that they didn't like opera or talking about politics.

Suddenly my dad looked up, his face puzzled and quizzical. "What's up, Paul? You look like you've lost a penny and found a pound."

"Other way round, love," said Mum.

"Oh yes, lost a pound and found a penny."

But by then the moment for talk was past, and they were back to their fish and chips, and slices of bread and margarine, and their cups of sweet tea, and so I left them there, and went to meet Maddy at the cinema of dreams.

And there is another way in which the scene before me is like a game of chess. There is a word, a truly excellent word. *Zugzwang*. It means coming to a place in the game, usually toward the end, where you are safe as long as you don't move. But it is your turn, and you must move. And if you move, you will lose.

    Zugzwang.

        Zugzwang.

            Zugzwang.

                      Zugzwang.

                          Zugzwang.

TWENTY-ONE

I got the bus into town. It was dark and the streetlights were on and it looked beautiful. I couldn't understand to begin with, but then I saw it was because of the fine rain falling, which made everything shine. Even the cars going by seemed to smile at me.

I tried to think of some things to say to Maddy. She was into books. I used to read books when I was younger— the Famous Five and Biggles, stuff like that. But then I stopped. I don't know why. In English we'd been reading a book called *Kes*, about a boy who has a pet kestrel. It wasn't exactly cheerful. The people are poor, and the main kid gets bullied, and then he gets caned by the teacher for something that wasn't his fault. His mum's a slut. The only good thing in his life is the kestrel. But his brother kills it. I liked the book a lot, but I didn't think it would impress Maddy, because it was just a school book, and even worse than that, it was what they gave you to read in the thicko class, because it was short. Maddy probably liked Shakespeare and that kind of thing. So, best steer clear of books.

Then I thought about something I'd read in a magazine while I was waiting at the dentist. It said that clever girls are always being told that they are clever, and pretty girls are always being told that they are pretty. So, if you want to impress them and make them like you, you should tell pretty girls that they are clever, and clever girls that they are pretty, because then they'll be surprised and think you've seen right into their soul. I liked the way Maddy looked, but I didn't think she was what most people would describe as pretty. But she was definitely clever. So it meant I had to say how nice she looked. I thought of different ways of saying it. I could tell her how nice her hair was, and her eyes. I could tell her I liked the way her body moved. But I wouldn't say it in a way that made it sound like that was all I was after—I mean, touching her and stuff.

It was a ten-minute walk to the cinema from the bus station. I was early, so I dawdled, looking at the shop windows. The rain was still in the air, but the drops were so tiny it was like a cold mist, and I loved the feel and taste of it and, even better, I always thought my hair looked best when it was wet from the rain.

I walked through the big department store on the main street, which was open late on Thursdays. A woman who looked so perfect she could have stepped straight out of a magazine smiled at me and asked if I wanted to try some aftershave. I suppose she was bored. I blushed, and let her spray some on me. It smelled nice—of lemons mixed with flowers. I'd never smelled like this before. It made me feel good, and I didn't mind that I was being followed by three store detectives.

There was a section where they sold amazing chocolates. You could select each one, and then they put them in a box for you and wrapped it up for you by hand. I checked my money. I had nearly forty pounds. It was all my money, taken from under the paper in my sock drawer. The tickets for the cinema were six pounds each. I decided to spend ten pounds on chocolates for Maddy, which would leave eighteen pounds for emergencies. A nice lady helped me choose, and when she asked if they were for my mum, I laughed and said no, and then blushed again, and she smiled at me, and I think she put extra effort into wrapping them up nicely, with the box first inside some cellophane, and then in thick pink paper, and then tied with a ribbon in a bow, and finally put into a paper bag with handles made of what looked like straw twisted into a kind of string. It felt like the most precious thing I'd ever held, even if there weren't very many chocolates in it.

I couldn't remember exactly where we'd arranged to meet—I mean, inside or outside. I went into the foyer and made sure she wasn't already there, checking every place she might have been. Then I waited outside for a while, but I got a bit cold, because by now my shirt was soaked. Back inside, I looked at the electronic board with the films scrolling across it in angular red letters. I didn't go to the cinema very often; in fact in my whole life I'd probably only been about five times, and I was looking forward to that part of the evening too. I thought about buying the tickets, but I was worried I'd choose the wrong film. Three different films started at eight. It was nearly that now, but I knew the adverts and trailers went on for ages. I walked up and down in the lobby, checking the big clock every few seconds as people, young and old, scruffy and smart, most laden with huge buckets of popcorn and paper cups of Coke the size of wastepaper bins, flowed around me.

I didn't have a mobile to call her, but that didn't matter, because I didn't know her number. At five past eight I began to get worried. At quarter past I began to feel sick. More films began at half past. Then half past went, and then nine o'clock. By then I was in a weird sort of trance, not really expecting her to show, not able to move in case I missed her. And if I left, then, well, all hope would be gone. If I stayed, there would always be some hope.

At half past nine people began to come out from one of the earlier sittings. I recognized one of them. It was Kirk. I was in the middle of the foyer, and there was nowhere to hide. At least I thought to hold the fancy bag behind my back.

"Hey, Paul," he said, in an unexpectedly friendly way. "What are you doing here?" He was with a girl. She was from the year below, and I didn't know her name, and Kirk didn't introduce her. She had straight black hair and black eyeliner and a black dress that went down to the floor. She was pretty, but she looked very young, and maybe Kirk was a bit ashamed of her and that's why he didn't introduce her. Or he was ashamed of knowing me.

"I was . . . I mean, I'm . . . I'm waiting for someone."

Then Kirk talked about the film they'd seen, discussing the cinematography and stuff I didn't really understand. It was a French film called *La règle du jeu*, showing as part of some arty movie season they had on. The little girl looked bored out of her skull.

Finally Kirk seemed to be ready to go. As a parting shot he asked, "Who is it you're waiting for, anyway?"

"No one," I said. "No one, really."

"No, go on, tell me," he said, and he sounded so friendly I thought that maybe I'd got him wrong, and that he was OK. And I felt like an idiot, standing there, obviously waiting for someone and then denying it. And so, stupidly, I told him.

"Maddy. We arranged to see a film."

His face did something odd—a quick smile, followed shortly by a look of grave concern.

"Maddy? But don't you know?"

"What?"

"She's with Shane tonight."

"What do you mean?"

"They're having an evening in, together."

Kirk said it slowly, sounding each word, making it sound like something special and different.

"I don't get it."

"Well, you know what his mum and dad are like—they let him do anything down there. They're really laid-back about it. As long as they use condoms. Reckon they'll bring them coffee and cigarettes on a tray afterward. Wish my parents were more like that."

"C'mon," said the girl. She was looking at her feet.

"Yeah, yeah," said Kirk, and gave me a *gee, what is it with these chicks* kind of look. Then he creased his face once again into an expression of concern. "You did know, didn't you? I mean, about Maddy and Shane? About them shagging?"

"Yeah, course," I said. "We were just going to see the . . . going to the cinema. There was a film . . . She must have . . ."

"Yeah, forgot or something. Women, eh!"

And then the girl gave him a playful slap and dragged him away, and he called out, "See you tomorrow," over his shoulder.

I waited till they were gone, and then went to sit on the steps leading up to the screens on level two. I sat there for about twenty minutes. To begin with I played over and over what Kirk had said. Then I imagined Shane and Maddy together. I could see them kissing, talking with their heads together. So close that they could stop talking and start kissing without having to move. And I heard them laughing at me, laughing at the geek who'd thought he could become just like them. Who maybe thought he could get into that tiny space between them, a space so tight that even a kiss could span it.

I threw the chocolates in the bin and walked home through the rain.

TWENTY-TWO

I got home at about eleven. My dad was still up, watching the telly.

"You're late, son," he said, his eyes flicking briefly from the screen to me, and then back again.

He didn't notice that I was soaked, that my teeth were chattering. Didn't notice that I'd left a trail of my guts all the way from the center of town.

I went and turned the telly off. My dad stood up and began to splutter. Turning the telly off wasn't something you did in our house. Then he saw my face and the spluttering stopped.

"It was all lies, wasn't it, Dad?"

"What are you talking about? Have you been drinking? Is that where you've been?"

"You're a liar, Dad, aren't you?"

"I don't know what you're talking about, son."

"About that big fight, all them years ago, up at Temple Moor."

My dad's face went suddenly blank and loose.

"Who have you been talking to?"

"What difference does that make? Tell me the truth. Were you a hero? Did you save those kids? Because I heard you shat yourself."

Then my dad slapped me across the face. He hadn't hit me for years. It stung, but I didn't flinch. I'd taken many worse slaps at school.

"I don't want to hear language like that in this house," he said, but already I saw that he had no real fight in him.

I wanted to hit him back. I didn't, but not because I was afraid to. The opposite. It didn't seem worth it.

"You ran, didn't you, Dad. You didn't stick up for anyone."

"It was a long time ago."

"Then you should have left it there. Why did you boast about it? Why did you lie?"

"Son, come here," he said, his voice broken, his face soft, melting, almost, from the bones. "I'm sorry I hit you—

let me . . ." And as he tried to touch me—hug me, I think—that's when I did hit him. Not really hit, more sort of shove. He fell back onto the settee, and I turned and ran up the stairs, and sat on the floor in my bedroom with my back to the door so no one could get in.

I stayed there all night like that, as wide awake as I've ever been in my life, and slowly the shirt dried upon my back.

But no. Players have not abandoned the board. A hand moves the piece. A knight is taken. And the knife is closer to me.

TWENTY-THREE

The next day at morning break I went to chess club. I thought it was a good place to be invisible. Mr. Boyle smiled when he saw me.

"Good man," he said, and introduced me to some of the other kids there. They were all ages—little ones from Year Seven, gangly Year Tens, fat boys from in between. There weren't any girls at all.

Mr. Boyle sat me down next to one of the young kids.

"Simon'll give you a game. Do you know how the pieces move?"

"Yeah."

Simon was too small for his clothes. When he wriggled, they stayed still. He had round glasses, and he stuck his tongue out when he concentrated.

In four moves I was checkmated.

He put his hand out to shake. I swept the pieces onto the floor with my arm and then stormed out. I saw Boyle's face as I left, puzzled, disappointed.

I wandered through the corridors for a few minutes, until the deputy head, Mr. Mordred, saw me.

"Outside, boy," he bellowed. He liked his school to be as free of kids as possible. If he'd had his way, we wouldn't be allowed in at all.

Outside I saw Shane and the freaks. It was easy to see them, because the playground was weirdly empty. Maddy was there, gazing out over the gypsy field. The wind moved her hair and she looked beautiful, and I hated her.

Billy caught my eye and waved, an idiot smile on his round stupid face. Shane glanced at me over his shoulder. Then Kirk spoke into his ear, and they laughed at something. I turned away and followed the line of the school building round a corner.

I knew who I was going to meet there. But it wasn't just Roth, Bates and Miller. It was all the nutters and hard kids and a crowd of insignificant hangers-on. They were talking, joking, messing with each other. No one paid much attention when I joined them. But then Roth pushed his way through to me.

"Good lad, good lad," he said, and cupped his palm around the back of my neck, drawing me in.

"I've got it," I said, the words falling out of me.

"You didn't need to tell me that," said Roth, close, close. "I could see straightaway. Anyone could. You look like a man, you look like a . . . like a *warrior*."

And because Roth treated me like his friend, I was everyone's friend, suddenly a part of this seething mass of fist and muscle and sinew. It felt good. Before, thinking about Maddy and Shane had made me weak, but now I was strong. I felt like we could do anything.

Roth was talking.

"What we don't want is for them to run for it. We want them all. We want them to *learn*. Every one of them. If they scatter, they'll say it was nothing. They'll say we didn't win. We've got to take away that option."

"But you can't stop 'em from running," said someone.

"We can."

"Not if we're on the gyppo field. They'll see us and shit themselves and leg it."

"Yeah, if we were all there. Course they would. That's them all over. But what if we're not all there? What if only some of us are there? At the beginning."

"You got a plan, Rothie? You have, haven't you!"

"They'll come from up there." Roth pointed across the gypsy field and up the hill. "They'll cross the road and come over the field."

"How do you know? What if they come the other way, along the road and round to the front?"

"Because they'll see something."

"What'll they see?"

"Bait."

Laughter then. The bright ones got it. The thick ones laughed because everyone else did.

"Bait, yeah, for the big fish. And how do you catch the big fish?"

"With a little fish."

"Come on then, Rothie, spit it out."

"OK, what we do is we get some kids to stand around in the field. All nice and smart in their blazers. That'll lead 'em on. They'll smell blood. They'll just come charging straight over. They'll think it's Christmas. But they won't see the rest of us, because we'll be down by the beck. When they get past us, then up we jump. We'll be behind them then, and there's nowhere for them to run."

He smashed his fist into his open palm. Hammer and anvil.

I could see that it was a good plan. The beck ran below the level of the field for most of the way, carving out a natural trench. Yeah, you could hide down there, waiting for the moment.

"But who's gonna be the bait? Because, like, bait gets eaten, dunnit?"

Roth smiled, and his black eyes glittered.

"Heroes. Volunteers. None of the big lads. We need some kids with nerves. They've got to stand there while the Templars charge them." Then he looked around at us, seeming to pause so that each kid felt his presence focused directly on him. "So we need some of you. There'll be more coming for the fight, but we need some of you to steady them."

Every kid there had imagined himself as part of the mob rearing up from the hidden beck, imagined the thrill of the charge, relished the shock and fear on the faces of their foes. But this was different. Waiting there while the Templars rushed upon them, praying that the others would come, but knowing that even if they did, then it might be too late.

Yes, bait gets eaten.

They shuffled and they looked at their feet.

"I'll do it," I said.

Some cheers. Relief, I think.

"That's it, that's the way. Good lad."

Roth held my shoulders and shook me. Part of me felt elated, proud. But another part, perhaps the coward part, perhaps the good part, my soul, recoiled. But Roth did not see that part, even though he had the ability to sniff out souls the way a pig sniffs out truffles.

"More, come on, more."

And a few others said they would. Dumb, fierce little kids who weren't afraid, or said they weren't afraid. Our job was to stand with the sheep, the ordinary kids who would come along to the fight to enjoy the spectacle. The kind of kids who might join in if we looked like winning.

"OK," said Roth, "let's see who else wants to play."

Then the crowd of us came from round the corner into the weak sunshine of the playground. Every face turned to meet us. Roth led the way, moving from one little group to the next, cajoling, enticing, persuading, threatening—whatever it took. And some kids joined in enthusiastically, glad to be called. And some were sullen, and some were afraid. But none were afraid of the future fight as much as they were afraid of the present Roth.

And then, at last, we came to Shane and the freaks. I'd seen them looking at us nervously as we made our way across the playground. Not Shane, of course. That little half-smile of his never left his lips. But Kirk looked like he had somewhere else he really needed to be, and fat Billy looked like he wanted to cry. I felt embarrassed that I'd ever wanted to be like them.

Roth stood in front of them. I was by his side.

"Any of these poofs up for it, you reckon?" said Roth.

"Nah," said Bates. "They'll be putting on their makeup. Then they might all have a little cry together."

"Shut up."

Of all people it was Serena who spoke up.

"Make me, you slut."

Then Serena stepped forward as if she was going to do just that, and she looked pretty awesome, with her purple lips and black hair, like something out of a vampire movie, and Bates shrank back from her. But not Roth. He put his hand almost gently on her arm and moved her out of the way. Almost gently, I said, but she still ended up on the floor.

Then things happened fast. Shane, not smiling now, not smiling at all, ran at Roth. For a second my heart leaped with joy, even though I was with Roth now. Shane was going to diminish Roth, he was going to do some trick. He knew tae kwon do or jujitsu or some such shit. That was where he got that amazing inner calm from.

But it was what Roth wanted; wanted above all else. Because of course he had always hated Shane, hated his indifference and detachment, his aloofness. What he hated most of all was that Shane presented us with an alternative, a different way of being. Roth wanted us to believe that all there was in the world was the fist, and the face into which it smashed. You could be on the side of the fist and do the hurting, or on the side of the face, and be crushed. The hurter or the hurt: there was no third way. Shane had floated free from that world. But that had to stop. He had to be tethered. So yes, Roth been waiting for this moment, the moment to hurt.

And there was a grace in the way Roth did it, because, I suppose, to be what Roth was, to achieve what he had achieved, you need that ability to make your body do just what you want it to do, to move in ways that conform to your ideas of harmony and beauty.

His hand, his right hand, moved from somewhere close to his left knee in a sweeping backhand slap, except that "slap" doesn't do justice to the meat and bone of it, and the flourish of the blow took his arm up and elegantly over his right shoulder. In memory, the blow must always follow its arc in slow motion, like the beating of a swan's wing in a documentary. But back here in the real world it was all speed, the whip and zip of it humming in the air. And there must have been a crack as it landed, a sound like something precious breaking, but I can't remember anything but that humming, and then the sight of Shane on his back, blood all over his face so you couldn't even see which part of him was bleeding.

And I heard someone calling my name, and I looked down and it was Maddy, and tears were streaming down her face, and she was saying something to me, asking for help or something, and part of me was glad that she was being made to suffer, and then the shadow of Bates fell over her and he spat thickly in her hair.

I told Bates not to do that, but the voice was only in my head. And then I saw Roth's face, its odd, satisfied vacancy as he stood over Shane, and then he began to fuss with the front of his trousers, and I remembered the Compson kid, and I knew what Roth was going to do. He was going to piss on Shane's face, the way he'd pissed on Compson's face.

Kirk and Stevie and Billy didn't know what to do— whether to try to help Shane, or attack us, or run away in case they were next, and so they stood there, lost, watching, desolate, their hands making ineffectual movements, as if they were bothered by summer flies.

That's when I found myself again, and I stepped

forward, and I said, "No," and put my hand on Roth's arm. And Roth turned on me, his face losing that pleasant vacancy, beginning its transition through irritation to rage, because couldn't I see that he was in the middle of something important here, part of the world's education? And deep in my heart I quailed.

But I had a reason.

"Boyle," I said, and nodded over his shoulder. The other kids all looked then, the Roth gang and the freaks. But not Shane.

Mr. Boyle was loping in our direction, his face red, his sparse beard bristling, the dirty tweed jacket flapping behind him like the wings of a hairy bat. The crowd scattered before him, kids flying in all directions. I didn't see Roth run, but he too disappeared. I was left with Shane and the others. Serena and Maddy were bending over him, and the boys were still standing aimlessly, not knowing what to do.

"What's . . . ? Who . . . ? What happened here?" Boyle looked around wildly, trying to understand what was going on.

"Don't know, sir."

I'm not sure who said it—one of the boys. It was the rule—the one rule nobody would break: you don't talk.

Boyle knelt by Shane's side, and took out a handkerchief and wiped the blood from his mouth. Shane's eyes were open, and he looked beyond Boyle to me.

"Who did this?"

"I fell, sir," said Shane, his voice wet and soft.

"Don't be stupid, boy. I saw something was going on. But there were too many of them in the way. Come on, who hit you? We need to stop this. It only takes one person to speak out."

But I knew Shane wouldn't say who had done it, because not even the saints like Shane would break the rule. It wasn't a rule like not chewing gum in class, but a law, a law of nature, like evolution or water boiling at 100 degrees. You don't break those kinds of laws. They're what we're made of.

"I fell, sir."

And Boyle looked away in despair. "You, Varderman, I'm asking you: what do you know about this?"

"I didn't see anything, sir."

I thought Boyle was going to burst. He uttered a series of spluttering noises, and then walked away, and then came back again and began helping Shane to get up.

"You're as much to blame as the others," he said to no one in particular. And then, in a softer tone, he added, "Come on, let's get you cleaned up. Then I'll drive you to the emergency room and we'll see if you need any stitches."

"I'm fine, sir."

"No you're not."

And then the two of them went away across the playground, heading for the stinking sick bay with its bucket of sand and its broken dummy they used to teach mouth-to-mouth, and the first aid kit with its empty box of Band-Aids.

TWENTY-FOUR

Silence, then.

I looked at the group. Stevie hunched over, shriveled, like a dying sunflower; Billy, his eyes wet with unspilled tears, hopeless without anything to smile about; Kirk, his mouth tight, his jaw clenched; Serena looking like a little girl; Maddy.

Maddy, so filled up with hate that she seemed radiant with it, like the electric glowing wire in a bulb, and to look on her burned that hate into you, the way the image of the red wire writes itself on you so you can see it even on the inside of your eyelids.

And she walked calmly up to me, and I closed my eyes, but still her burning image was there, and she said a word, and then she spat in my face—not the thick phlegm of Bates, but the spraying spittle of someone who had never spat like that before—spitting as a message, I mean. And when I opened my eyes, they were gone and I was alone in the playground and the word echoed in my head.

Traitor.

Traitor.

Traitor.

The shadow over my shoulder is growing. I shouldn't be worried about it, not with the hot tongue of metal flickering in front of me. The shadow is blunt. The shadow is soft. Blunt and soft cannot hurt. Blunt and soft cannot go into you. But the metal tongue goes into you as if you wanted it, as if that was what you'd always wanted, the tongue of it inside you. So why is the shadow making me afraid? Why is it pulling me away from the danger in front? And if my concentration slips, then the knife slips, closer. Oh God, closer.

TWENTY-FIVE

Billy found me in the library at lunchtime.

It took me a while to realize he was there. I'd been thinking about a time when I was small. Maybe six or seven, something like that. My parents had some friends who had kids the same age as me. We were having a picnic all together down in the gypsy field, which sounds mad, but on a sunny day it could be quite nice. There were a few places where the fold of the ground meant you couldn't see any houses, and with the sound of the beck running in the background it almost felt like you were in the real countryside. We had ham sandwiches and sausage rolls and jam fritters, which were actually just jam sandwiches deep-fried in batter, but I loved them. I played in the beck with the other children. We had on jelly-shoes to guard against the broken glass and rusty wire, and we waded in the brown water while our parents drank beer and wine and got red faces in the sun.

There was a girl called Bethany who had the curliest hair you ever saw, and I remember holding her hand while she balanced on an old fridge that was thrown away in the beck, and the other children made fun of us for holding hands, but I didn't mind because I liked Bethany and her curly hair.

And I think I was reaching out my hand to touch Bethany's curly hair when Billy sat himself down heavily opposite me, filling the space I wanted to gaze into.

"I was looking for you," he said in a heavy whisper, although there was no one else in the library.

"You found me."

It was hard being unfriendly to Billy. But hard is what I'd become.

"Kirk told me."

"Told you what?" I made my voice as empty as I could, and my eyes avoided his.

"What he did."

"What makes you think I care what Kirk did?"

"Not just *did*—what he did to *you*."

"Kirk didn't do anything to me."

"You think?"

"Kirk's nothing to me. None of you are."

"You don't fool me. I saw what happened at break. You tried to hide it, but I saw."

"Don't know what you're talking about."

"Out there. I saw you stop Roth. He was going to do something terrible, and you stopped him."

"I just warned him that Boyle was coming."

"No. That wasn't it. I was watching. You stopped him first, then you saw Boyle. Boyle was just an excuse."

"You don't know what you're talking about. Why should I care if Roth pissed on Shane, or any of you?"

"Will you listen to me? I know you're not like this. We were together just now in the dining hall. We were all a bit shocked, you know, because of Shane. And Kirk was talking, the way he does. He said he saw you at the Odeon, waiting for Maddy. He said it was why you'd gone over to that lot, to the thugs."

"I'm not listening to this."

"You are listening. You've got to listen. He was taking the piss, saying what a loser you are. He said that's why you turned against us, that's why you became one of them, one of the shits, just because Maddy stood you up. He said that you'd shown what you were really like. Said we should never have let you in. And all the time Maddy had this look on her face, like *What are you talking about?* Then she said she'd never stood you up, that she couldn't have, because she didn't even realize you had a date."

"I'm not saying we did."

"But that's what you thought, isn't it? That's why you were waiting around at the Odeon?"

I said nothing, but I couldn't stop the shame from showing.

"Well, she hadn't understood—whatever, I don't know. But I'm telling you, she wasn't faking. She didn't stand you up. It was news to her that you two had a date. So then Kirk said you were a psycho and had imagined the whole thing, and that anyway Maddy was out of your league."

"Yeah, well, thanks, Billy, that's really cheered me up. Is that why you came here? Mission accomplished. Now get lost."

"I haven't finished yet. Because then that little Year Nine girl of his—Lucy, I think her name is—showed up with a plate of plain boiled rice 'cos that's all she eats. And she sort of blurted out what Kirk had said, about Shane and Maddy screwing, and Kirk tried to shut her up. Then they had a row, and she said he was always going on about Maddy, and if she was so wonderful, why didn't he go out with her? And he said, yeah, why not, so she stormed off, leaving her rice behind. But we'd twigged by then. It was all Kirk. He'd said it all out of spite."

"I don't even know what you're saying. Don't know and don't care."

"Listen to me! Kirk was lying when he said that Maddy and Shane were together. I mean, together like that. They aren't. They never could be."

"What do you mean?"

177

"How could you not know?"

"Know what?"

"Shane. Maddy. Couldn't happen."

"Of course it could. I've seen her look at him. Kirk's right. I was stupid to think . . . Just get lost, will you, Billy, I've stuff to do."

"He's gay."

"What?"

"Shane's gay."

Then came the sort of silence that pounds in your ears. And then I laughed. And then I cursed. And then I said, "You're taking the piss."

"You know what this school is like. Do you think I'd joke about it? Imagine being gay here. Imagine what would happen to you if it got out. Imagine what that does to you, inside. Maddy's got a brother who . . . Well, that's for her to tell you. Anyway, she understood better than anyone. She was a shoulder for him to cry on. And maybe she felt things for him, I don't know. Would be a bit weird, if you ask me, but that's not the point."

"So what *is* the point?"

Everything Billy had said made a kind of sense, and maybe it should have cheered me up, but it didn't. I was too confused, too heartsick. I didn't know what to think about Shane being gay. It made me feel queasy and embarrassed. It made me think in a different way about things he'd said and done. I know it shouldn't, but it did. And the knowledge that

Maddy hadn't deliberately stood me up got lost in the fact that she hadn't noticed me enough even to realize that I'd asked her out.

There was too much, so I blanked it out, made it go away.

"The point? *The point?*" said Billy, almost shouting now, his arms waving around for emphasis. "The point is that you don't have to get mixed up in all that bullshit after school. The stupid fight. Acting like Roth's right-hand man. We can just forget about the past couple of days, get on with life. And you never know, you and Maddy—"

"Shut up about Maddy." I surprised myself with the concentrated spite in my voice.

"OK, whatever . . ."

"It's too late."

"It's never too late."

"Everything's . . . in place."

"So what? Just don't go."

"You don't understand."

"Damn right I don't understand."

"Go away, Billy. Go away and play your silly games. Pretend that your lives are interesting. Pretend that you're special. Pretend there's some great tragic drama that you're part of. You lot are pathetic. You think you're better than everyone else, you think you've got more depth. But you're not deep, you're stupid. You don't get it—don't get how the world works. You read books and you talk about them but you never see what's around you. Well, Roth does. Roth sees everything. And you're not even much good at being a freak. You're too fat and you laugh too much."

And then smiling Billy's round face, so wrong for a freak, so right for a clown, suddenly looked gaunt, and it was as if I was seeing through the flesh to the skull beneath. He got up slowly, like an old man, and I felt sorry for what I'd done.

"Look, Billy," I said, "I appreciate you coming here, saying what you said. But things are different now, and that's all there is to it. Anyway, how's Shane?"

When he answered, his voice was empty.

"Maddy called him. A couple of stitches. He'll be back in school in no time."

And then he was gone, his bulk swaying its way into the corridor, like an old-time sailing ship leaving a small harbor.

TWENTY-SIX

I had geography with Mr. Boyle in the afternoon. His heart wasn't in the lesson, and he didn't even bother to stop the kids talking among themselves. He just droned away, pausing sometimes to write stuff on the whiteboard in his unreadable handwriting. As usual, Roth and Bates and Miller were behind me, but they didn't throw chewing gum today. We were on the same side now.

Despite the boring lesson, you could sense the excitement build up as we got nearer the time of the fight. It was an excitement I didn't share. The anger I'd felt about Maddy and Shane was gone. What was left behind was a kind of gray sludge. Not really what you need to get in the mood for a fight.

I'm trying to find the right word for what I felt; trying to find a big word, a good word. But maybe the right word is a simple one: I felt sad. My time of being a freak was over. For a while I'd almost become one of Roth's nutters, but that was never going to work. I wasn't hard enough, and I didn't enjoy other people's pain. But there was no way I was going to back out of the battle. I didn't want to live with the shame of it, like my dad had done, hiding it beneath lies and bluster. I'd said I'd be there, so be there I would.

"Stay behind, will you, Varderman."

The lesson was over, and Boyle was talking to me.

I heard a hiss from behind.

"Make sure you're there, or we'll come looking for you."

I turned, ignoring Mr. Boyle. "I'll be there."

When the rest of the class were gone, I went and stood by Boyle's desk. He was writing something, and made me wait for a couple of minutes. Finally he put down his pen. It was a chewed Bic biro, same as a kid would use.

"What's going on, Varderman?"

"Don't know, sir."

"Do you think I'm an idiot, Varderman?"

"No, sir."

"Then tell me what's happening. Because something is. The whole school's buzzing with it."

"Nothing's happening, sir. It's going-home time, sir, that's all."

Then Mr. Boyle picked up his pen and wrote some more. I twisted and squirmed and fidgeted, terrified in case Roth thought I was trying to get out of the fight.

"I was talking to Shane on the way to the ER," he said after a while. "Oh, don't worry, he wouldn't tell me anything either. But he said that he thought you needed help. He said he thought that you could do things with your life."

"It's not up to him what I do with my life, sir."

Then Boyle looked at me properly for the first time. "I used to go to school with your dad, you know."

"I know, sir."

My dad had told me. He laughed when I told him I had Mr. Boyle for geography. He said everyone thought Boyle was a joke, because he was brainy and clumsy and was always falling over his feet. My dad said they called him "Boyle on the bum."

"He helped me once. There was a scrap, and the big lads were getting rough, and your dad helped me and a few others to get away. It was up at Temple Moor. I was only there because that's where I lived. I was scared stiff. But your dad was pretty cool. He wasn't stupid enough to stay for the fight, but he didn't just run off and leave us. It's a long time ago. I don't know why I'm telling you this." He looked at me again, holding my eye. "Your dad, he was OK."

I knew why he was telling me this. He knew that there was going to be a fight. He knew I was mixed up in it.

"Sir, can I go now?"

Another pause. More writing.

"No, Paul. I'm giving you a detention."

"Detention, sir?" I said, outraged. "But I haven't done nothing."

"Anything, Paul."

"What, sir?"

"You haven't done *anything*, not nothing."

"I know, sir, but, sir . . ."

"Go and sit back at your desk. Write me an essay. Write me an essay about history. About what we can learn from history."

But I didn't go back to my desk. I gave Mr. Boyle one last look—a look that was meant to say: *Sorry, and I understand what you're trying to do, and I think that maybe you're OK too*, but probably didn't get any of that across, and then I ran out of there way too fast for him to catch me or do anything more than utter an exasperated bellow of "Varderman, come back."

This boy who is coming to hurt me. I know you. How could I not have seen it before? It is a relief to know that I am not to be killed by a stranger. I test to see if knowing him, knowing the truth of him, can help me to stop his progress. Because knowledge is power, and power is what I need. Power to stop the world. Or, if not stop, then to divide the world into that infinite number of steps. Half, quarter, eighth, sixteenth . . . I know you, and you will never reach me.

TWENTY-SEVEN

It was OK—nothing had happened yet. There were at least forty kids in the gypsy field, all clustered around Roth. The drizzle was steady now, filling the air, but there weren't many coats. Just wet kids, hair plastered down on their white foreheads. As I got nearer, I could see that there were two distinct groups. The first group was made up of the tough kids from our year, and the hardest from the two years below. Not the kind of kids you'd want to get on the wrong side of. The bullies and thugs and meatheads. The ones who took your dinner money and knelt on your chest and spat in your face. Not nice boys. Not nice boys at all.

And then there were the others. Smaller, mostly, but with a few gangly beanpoles and some roly-poly fatties. These were the ones who'd come because they'd been told to, or who didn't know what was really going on, or who thought it was their only chance to make a mark, to worm their way into the approval of the top dogs. Some looked frightened already, and others were trying to work themselves up into a bloodlust, but it still appeared fake, like little kids playing at war.

"Paul, good," said Roth, and drew me to him, through the mass, as if by sheer force of gravity. "You've got a mission. You're the most important person here." And while he was saying it, while he was murmuring into my ear, pressing me close, I believed him.

"You know what to do?"

I nodded uncertainly.

"One more time. You keep this lot here"—he gestured toward the bait—"you keep this lot together, over there, where the beck bends back."

He pointed to where the beck made a U-shape. Once the Templars came, there'd be no way for us to escape—we'd be completely trapped against the beck. But then, so would they. That was the idea.

"I don't want any runners," Roth said to me, but loud enough for the others to hear. "Anyone runs, and the plan fails. If the plan fails, I'm gonna hurt someone. Have you got that?"

I nodded.

"And you know what you've got, if you need it?"

Again I nodded, ashamed, excited.

"Right then, quick, before they get here." And then Roth began to turn to the hard kids.

"Wait," I said.

Roth turned back slowly to me. "What?"

"It's going to be bad if you don't . . . if you don't come."

Roth smiled. "Don't come? We'll come. And we've got some surprises."

Then Roth opened his jacket. A big black handle stuck out of the top of the inside pocket of his blazer. And the pocket itself was almost bursting at the seems. There was something big in there, bigger than a knife. And around him, the other thugs also moved clothing and showed some of what they had. There were metal bars and chains and rocks and knives. The kids I was there to lead saw this, and they shouted and cheered, but I felt sick.

"Anything else?" Roth said to me.

I shook my head, and walked with the rest of the bait—about twenty kids altogether—over the uneven wet grass of the gypsy field to our place.

Looking over my shoulder, I saw Roth and the others stalk off until they reached the part of the beck that dipped beneath the level of the field, and one by one they dropped down out of sight, like devils returning to the underworld.

Despite the fact that there were still about twenty of us left, it suddenly felt very lonely. And now I looked at them again, the kids I was with seemed even more insignificant and scrawny than before. There weren't many kids from my year—the hard ones were all hidden down by the beck with Roth, and the rest were clever or cowardly enough to know not to get mixed up in this. I'm not tall for my age, just average, but I saw that I was the biggest there. It made me feel strange, and it took me a few seconds to realize that it was a good strange, not a bad one.

I felt a tug at my sleeve.

"Do you know what's happening?"

I looked down. It was the annoying Year Eight urchin whose ball I'd booted away. The same one Roth had been about to grate against the wall before Shane saved him. It seemed like years ago.

"What?"

"I was at the back. I couldn't hear. Where are we going?"

"Why ask me?"

The kid's face stared up at me. The other faces were also turned to me. I had a powerful urge to wave my hand at them and leave, walking away across the field—away from them, away from the school, away from Shane, away from Maddy, away from everything. But something inside me knew that you can't walk away from stuff like that, that it follows you and ruins wherever you go. And there was something else. These pathetic losers needed me.

"What was your name again?"

"Skinner."

"Well, Skinner, that's where we're going."

I pointed to the loop in the stream, twenty meters ahead.

"And what do we do when we get there?"

"We wait."

"What are we waiting for?"

The others were listening in now. I wondered what Roth had told them.

"The Temple Moor lot are going to come across the field. They'll see us and charge. We stand there until Roth and the others arrive."

"Oh." The kid thought for a minute. "But then they'll be behind them."

"Yeah."

"And we'll be in front of them."

"That's right."

"But there'll be nothing in between us and them."

"What did you think was going to happen? Why did you come here, anyway?"

"Everyone said that we had to. They said it was the honor of the school. Is that not right?"

I didn't know what to say to him. But something was needed.

"Look, it'll be OK. When Roth and the others attack them, the Templars'll ignore us and try to fight against them. That's if they don't just run for their lives."

Well, it was possible.

We reached the place, and I found that I was leading them.

"What now?" said someone.

"I've already told you. We wait."

"But should we get ready or something?"

I stared at the rabble. It looked like a decent belch would blow them all down. Roth could have picked them all up and crumbled them like a bouillon cube. I was torn between a kind of contempt and pity. But their young faces were all upon me. I had become their Messiah, their hope.

I went through them, picking out the bigger ones, the ones who looked like they might be able to take care of themselves.

"OK, you lot," I said, "you're in front."

I lined them up, facing away from the beck.

"The rest of you, you're to stay back here."

"I'm not going at the back," said Skinner.

"That's up to you," I replied, half annoyed, half impressed by his gumption. "Stand wherever you want."

Then I went and checked out the beck. The banks here went straight down, without any kind of path or flat bit along the edge. It was a half-meter drop into the water. The stream itself was quite strong, flowing smooth and brown. I didn't know how deep the water was. A meter maybe. In an emergency we could escape across it, but it wouldn't be nice.

"I can see something," said one of the boys.

We all looked up the hill. Yes, there they were. A

purple cloud. Couldn't tell how many yet, but it was plenty. I glanced over to where Roth and his mob were lurking. I saw a head bob up, stay for a moment and then duck down again. He'd seen them too.

The kids around me began to fidget.

"I've got to go home," said one kid. He was the smallest one there. "Me tea's ready. Me mum'll kill me."

"You can't. You heard what Roth said. You want him to hurt you?"

"But I don't like it here."

Someone laughed mockingly, and a rough hand pushed the little kid in the back.

"Anyone else want to go home?" I asked.

A couple of them looked at each other, but then there was a general shaking of heads.

"OK, you," I said to the little one. "The only way you can leave without Roth seeing you is to go through the beck."

"No chance," he said, wide-eyed with terror. "There's rats . . ."

A lot of the kids were scared of the beck. Scared of the filth in it and the rats, and the stuff you couldn't see under the surface.

"Well, you'll have to stay then."

And then the tears started to roll down his face, and he began to whimper.

It was turning into a disaster. If this kid really lost it,

then there was no telling what effect it might have on the others. I grabbed him by the jumper.

"Shut up," I said. "Get on my back."

"What?"

"Up. Get up."

Then, with him pushing and me pulling, I got him on my back and stepped down into the water. The kid weighed nothing—I've eaten bags of chips that had more substance—but the current almost whipped my legs from under me, and I stumbled and I felt the boy cling to me, the way you sometimes see a baby monkey holding on to its mother's back. But I steadied myself, and we were set.

The water was up to my knees. I could feel the ooze and slime under my trainers. I walked on, grunting with each step. Then the water was over my knees, and lapping against the kid's feet. But it was fine, we were getting there. Until the next time I put my foot down, and it seemed as if it would never reach the bed of the stream, and I staggered and lurched. The boy clung even tighter, his arms around my neck, cutting off the air. The water was around my waist, pulling me, nagging me, urging me to fall. But we did not fall. I tottered on and reached the far bank. I didn't have the strength to climb out with the boy on my back, so I twisted and threw him down.

"Hey!" he yelled. "Careful!"

"Piss off home," I said. And the kid, without saying thanks, ran scampering away, tripping and falling a couple of times in the rough grass. And then, when he felt safe, he turned, screamed a curse, and threw up his fingers at me in a frenzy of Vs.

I suppose I should have been offended or angry or something, but I found myself smiling at first and then laughing so much I almost fell over on my way back across the beck.

TWENTY-EIGHT

The other kids all looked at me like I was mad when I came out of the beck. Understandable, really, as I was draped in pondweed and coated with green scum, laughing, dripping, stinking from the mud and filth. But they were also afraid. I looked beyond them and saw why. The Templars were now only about five hundred meters away. They'd come off the road and were on the gypsy field. I couldn't see their faces properly, but I could sense their pumped-up frenzy, and their unity, and their battle joy.

Some of them had taken off their ties and wrapped

them, bandana-like, around their heads. It sounds stupid now, but it had an effect on us. It was creepy and savage, and it made me think that maybe Roth was right about them being barbarians.

"Take it easy, boys," I said, feeling the fear and the nervousness of the kids around me. "Just stay together and we'll be OK. Keep to your lines. You big lads in front, the little ones behind. Keep tight. It's fine—they'll never reach us. Remember, Roth's just over there. He's watching. He can see them. He'll be here."

I was babbling, but I thought words would help.

And now we heard them for the first time, a ragged shouting, not yet the single voice of the mob, but individuals yelling insults.

How many?

So many.

At least fifty of them. And it wasn't like our lot. Our lot might amount to almost fifty, but over half were waifs and strays. The kids in the Temple Moor mob looked huge, not like boys at all, but men.

Closer now, and I could see Goddo leading them. I felt the boys on either side of me bunch closer. Roth said that they would charge straight across the gypsy field as soon as they saw us, but they didn't do that. They came quite slowly. Perhaps Goddo suspected something. Perhaps he was just enjoying it so much he wanted it to last.

A hundred meters away, they stop. Goddo is talking to

his mob. He raises his arms as if he's trying to calm them down. And he walks ahead of the others, toward us.

He's close enough now for me to see his eyes. And for him to see mine. There is the moment of recognition, and then he smiles, the smile huge, open, almost friendly.

"Hey, it's the messenger boy!"

The others who were with him back in the park begin to laugh and point. Then Goddo becomes serious.

"Who are these . . . *children* you're with, messenger boy?"

And so I'm going to have to speak. No one told me that I would have to speak. It isn't why I'm here.

But I speak.

"Why don't you go back, Goddo? You don't belong down here. If you go now, there won't be any trouble."

"Good words, messenger boy. But you know why I'm here. And it isn't for you and these beck rats. Where is he?"

Where indeed? The Temple Moor kids aren't close enough for the trap to close. Roth is waiting, waiting, still dangling us, the bait, before the jaws.

"We're not here to fight you," I say.

"I can see that," laughs Goddo. "You won't be doing any fighting. You might do some hurting, but not fighting. Where's the man? Tell me the truth."

I don't know what makes me turn round then. I must have heard something, but I can't remember it now. But I turn and see, of all people, Kirk, my enemy, standing on the far side of the beck. He looks back at me and smiles. There is something in his hand. Beyond him I can see other figures coming, a tall one, a fat one, but then I focus on Kirk again. The thing in his hand: half a brick. He looks at me, an enigmatic smile on his lips. And then he draws back his hand and throws the brick. I flinch, thinking he's throwing the brick at me. But it sails high over my head.

I spin back to the Temple Moor kids. The brick descends. It's a good shot. It hits the boy next to Goddo in the head. He falls, his hands to his face, red blood flowing between his fingers.

What happens next is sometimes fast and sometimes slow and sometimes both at the same time. There is a roar. The whole mass of them now swell and surge and boil toward us, like the billowing hot ash and gas from a volcano. There is a sort of frightened scream from the children around me, and I feel them cringe toward me, as if I can save them. I glance quickly behind me, and see Kirk running, safe on his side of the stream. And then I look over to the hidden Roth and his battalions. And yes, at last, they are coming too, jumping up now from their hiding place.

But it is late.

It is too late.

And something else I notice. They are not all coming. Some have hung back, others have moved only slowly toward us, as if waiting to see what will happen, ready to turn and run if running looks like the thing to do.

But there is nowhere for *us* to run. The beck encloses

us on three sides, the enraged Templars are on the fourth. I put out my hands, trying to reassure the children near me by touch. But I understand now that I have done a terrible thing, that I allowed my own anger and despair to blind me to the damage I might do.

"Paul!"

I turn round. Billy and Stevie are already in the beck, Serena and Maddy behind them on the far bank.

"Send them across. The kids."

It's Stevie talking, looking more alive than I've ever seen him, his spiky elbows and knees working. I start to throw the youngest kids into the water. Billy and Stevie shunt, carry, shove them on to Maddy and Serena. Six, eight, ten, splashing across, some laughing, most terrified. But there's no time.

Goddo's mob are here.

And Roth also. It's a three-way collision. Us, the Templars, Roth and his handful of close mates.

Roth hits them from the side. Goddo hasn't seen him, so the impact is dramatic. Suddenly limbs are flailing every-where. Fists moving, punching air, punching faces, punch-ing air again.

A Templar kid, taller than me, wider than me, puts his hand on my face and pushes me back, back toward the brown flowing water. But my face is still slippery from the slime and the pondweed, and the hand slides off, and he falls forward, carried by his momentum, and it is easy to shove him into the beck, his hands flapping at the water.

Then a punch hits the side of my head. I am conscious of the weight of it but I don't register the pain. I fall to my knees and I look up, and the boy, his mouth a lipless line of hate, is going to punch me again. But then a savage creature leaps at him, feet, knees, arms, hands all frantically beating. It is the Year Eight urchin, Skinner. He is fierce, but the Templar kid is too strong for him and throws him down. He raises his foot to stamp on Skinner's face, and so I charge at him, and my head hits his stomach and steals his air, and he makes a sound, half groan, half gasp.

I take a second to look around me. This is the terrible equation, impossible to understand. Everywhere there are individual scraps, kids clawing and punching at each other. Gouging, scratching, slapping. Nothing glorious here, no beauty or grace in it, just humans brought to the level of animals. But I see a space and pull Skinner with me. We have somehow escaped from the circle of hell. Skinner's face has blood on it, but I don't think it's his.

"You're bleeding," he says, and I feel behind my ear, and there is blood on my hand, which makes me laugh.

"Run home now," I shout at Skinner, but not using those words, using bad words, and this time he does exactly what I tell him. I meant to thank him, but there was no time, and now I never will.

And then I look for the other small kids, the ones who had been in my care, the ones I should have protected. Most have escaped back across the beck, and I don't even think about them. A couple are cowering down, hunkering into the grass like leverets, but they also seem safe, for now.

But everywhere there is the horror. Weapons have come out: blunt clubs, rocks, wood, chains. But not yet knives.

That is when I see Bates entwined with Mickey, Goddo's spiky-haired lieutenant. And in another place, another time, it might look as though they were lovers, not fighters, because they hold each other so close, and their gazes are fixed so intently on each other, and each has his hands on the other's face, feeling for its tender parts. And now I watch with horror as Bates opens his mouth and bites Mickey's cheek, scraping and gnawing at it like a cannibal, and I would have stopped it if I could.

But then I see Roth, and once I see him, it is impossible to look anywhere else.

His face is transformed, and shines with a cool silvery metallic radiance, like moonlight or mercury. Oh, but he is suddenly beautiful—beautiful like Lucifer was said to be beautiful. His arms enclose his enemies and he crushes them, and two fall before his feet. A tall red-haired boy holding a thick plank of wood rushes toward him, spittle and noise coming from his mouth. There is a long nail in the end of the wood. Roth's movement is so perfect it seems more like music than solid form, and the wood and the nail go into the place where he was, which is now simple space, and the wood plows the ground and Roth's foot breaks the wood, and his knee smashes up into the face of the boy. Two more punches, each slashing high to low, and two more Temple Moor kids are down, and one is holding his face and crying and the other one does not even move.

But then I see a change come over Roth's face, and the change makes me shudder. Roth's brilliance has blinded me to something else. But now he sees it, and I see it too.

There are so few of us.

He sees that he is with Bates, who has somehow untangled himself from his lover, his meal, and Miller, and two, three, four other kids from our school. But there are still so many Templars. And now Roth's face loses that evil beauty and becomes grim and ugly, because perhaps at some level he has realized that what lies in store for him is defeat, and then the dreadful things that come with defeat. And maybe you can be noble in defeat, but you can't be beautiful.

But still, a kick this time, straight out and into the groin of a boy, and another backhanded, lip-bursting slap. And only Bates and Miller now are with him and, strangely, me.

How did I come to be here?

Or was it that he came to me?

"You've got it," he says to me—not a question. "Because now is the time."

I cannot help putting my hand to my pocket, where the knife waits for me. It would be easy, then, to take out the knife, to answer his call, to answer *its* call. But I close my ears and I shake my head, and his mouth goes hard with frustration and anger. He is panting, and a film of sweat covers his face. I have let him down.

But before he can say anything else, a voice rises above the clamor.

"ROTH!"

Goddo.

And Roth smiles again, as if this is what he has been waiting for. And the world stops and watches.

The two of them are alone now, three meters apart, close enough to spit, if you have the wind. A sort of ragged circle has formed. More than thirty Templars on one side, me, Miller, Bates on the other, with more broken kids on the ground, silent or weeping.

"You killed my little girl," says Goddo. "You killed my baby. You're gonna be sorry."

I don't know what to make of Goddo. In some ways he's an impressive guy. He has grace and power and he seems more human than Roth. But maybe that is also his failing, because he showed his weakness when he talked like that about his dog, talking like he wanted to cry about it. And I feel no sympathy for Goddo, because of what he did to me with the jaws of that dog.

Then Roth says some things that I can barely bring myself to tell you. Some of the things he says are about what he did to the dog, and some of the things are about Goddo. And then he calls Goddo the thing you can't call a person, not now.

"Nigger," he says.

And I know why he says it, and maybe even Goddo

knows why he says it, but that doesn't make any difference, because now he does just what Roth wants.

He charges.

And I know what Roth will do next. A tiny, almost imperceptible feint one way, and then a swerve to the other. Goddo will flail at space and Roth will put him down.

But that isn't happening. Goddo is fast. As fast as Roth. That has never been the case before. Not fast enough so that Roth's move fails completely, but fast enough so that his fist catches Roth just on the point of the chin. Another centimeter and it would have missed. But the chin. The chin. Roth's head is so massy, so solid, that almost anywhere else and he would have laughed at the punch. But no one laughs at a punch on the point of their chin. In a street fight you don't want to punch a kid on the chin, because it means you'll break your fingers like dry sticks. And maybe Goddo's fingers are broken, but it doesn't matter. Roth stops. Stops like a clock when you take out the battery. His eyes look troubled for a moment, and then cloud, and then he falls to one knee.

The Templars scream with joy, their tension and fear suddenly released, like pigeons exploding out of a loft.

For a second Goddo looks like he doesn't realize what's happened. He stands back, suspecting a trick, a trap. And then, when Roth keeps his head low, staring at the ground as if he's lost something vital there, Goddo moves closer to him, his head high, a sneer on his lips.

"Call me that again," he whispered, meaning what Roth said before, the terrible thing.

And now Roth looks up at him, and even though the light is dim in his eyes, the Templars all take a step back. Except Goddo. Goddo takes a step forward.

Mistake.

Roth, still unsteady, lunges, hurling himself at Goddo's legs. The two are down together. Goddo hammers away at the back of Roth's head, but Roth worms his way higher, his big hands reaching, clawing for Goddo's neck. Goddo is a tough kid. No one else could keep Roth this busy for this long. But Roth is Roth, and no one can beat him. He's on top now, and a sigh comes from the Templars. It doesn't matter that the battle up till now has been theirs: all that counts is this fight between the champions.

And Goddo must lose now.

Roth has his knee on Goddo's chest. A hand is at his throat, and Goddo can only wave and flap his arms like a dying bird. It is over. I can see the light die in the eyes of the Templars. They want no more of this fight. They will go home now, dragging their injured and their humiliated with them.

Except that Roth is not satisfied. He is feeling with his free hand inside his jacket. And I remember now that wide shape beneath the black handle. With a shout he pulls it from his pocket. It is a fat-bladed meat cleaver, its edge ground razor-sharp. He flourishes it above his head. He is going to kill Goddo with it.

I realize then that I have to move, have to stop this atrocity. But Roth changes his grip, and I hesitate. Now he holds out one of Goddo's hands against the soil. He scrabbles and twists until a finger is isolated. And then up goes the cleaver again. For a second it pauses, bright against the mackerel sky. And then it falls, and I have done nothing to stop it.

Except that it doesn't fall, or rather its fall is caught.

Roth looks round, looks up, and his face is filled with mystery, disbelief, utter bafflement. This was something he had never expected.

Miller.

Neatly, Miller takes the cleaver from Roth's hand and hurls it toward the beck. As it turns slowly in the air, I half believe that a hand will burst from the water to catch it, but it enters uncaught and soundless.

"Shouldn't have called him that," said Miller, his face expressionless. And then he just walks away.

Why did Miller betray Roth like that? Is it really a betrayal when what you are betraying is evil? Maybe he'd been waiting for this moment for years. Maybe it was just a whim. But I think there comes a time when the corrosive burning works down to the part that won't burn, that won't corrode, and Miller had reached that part, his core. And when he reached it, he found that there was still something noble there, even if it expressed itself in an act of treachery.

Now I turn back to the fight. Roth is lost, his arm still stuck up in the air as if he is answering a question in class. Ridiculous. He looks ridiculous. Who could have thought such a thing? And Goddo rises up from under him, and all the Templars, freed now from the enchantment of defeat, close upon him, and all I can see is the ripple of arms and legs working, like a soft machine.

But there is no time to understand the soft machine, no chance to explore how it works, because a shape is rushing toward me. Bates, in a blind panic, runs like a rat toward the beck. He pushes me and I fall back. I get up to see that not all the Templars are gathered around Roth.

Mickey, his face covered in blood, a flap of skin hanging loose from his cheek, is alone. No, not quite. Didn't Roth once say to me that when you've got a knife, you're never alone? And in his hand is not that penknife of his, but a cheap, long-bladed kitchen knife.

I don't know if in some way his mind has mixed up Bates and me, or if he just wants to hurt someone, and I am easier to reach than Bates, who has fled across the brown beck, or Roth, who is still caught in the workings of the soft machine, the Templars on him the way vultures cover a carcass.

Whatever the reason, Mickey fixes his eyes on me and begins to run, holding the knife. For a second I think about taking out *my* knife, the beautiful killing blade that Roth gave me. But I have already made that decision. And anyway, there is no time.

This is it *now*, this is really it. I cannot keep him there any longer, cannot even slow him. He pours toward me like water, and now I can hear the sound he makes, a high wailing sound, more like misery than rage.

I wish that I had let him put his knife into me. If he had put his knife into me, I would not have died. But I had learned things from Roth. I had learned the simple trick of moving one way and then another. And I cannot deny that the adrenaline-rushing joy of battle entered me. It is what biology and history have given us. This surge of chemicals that turns us from kind things to cruel.

It is easy. I do what Roth could not do to Goddo. I move and catch Mickey's arm as he passes me, and twist it behind his back, and take it from him, take the knife. But Mickey is a tough kid, and strong for his size, and I find that I cannot hold him. He wriggles and fights and somehow manages to bite my hand so that I drop the knife, and then we scramble together, rolling in the mud. And I am aware that I am fighting with a Temple Moor kid, and that we are surrounded by other Templars, and I become frightened for my life for the first time. And fear is a strange thing, because it makes you love life, and cling to it. So I gain new strength, and in spite of his writhing and twisting, I finally have him down, and I put the knife to his throat.

Now, you must be clear about this, absolutely clear. This is the most important thing. I wasn't going to cut him. I wasn't going to touch him with the knife. I only wanted him to be still.

And he is. Perfectly still at last. His eyes are huge and white. I will climb off him now, and run, run home to my mum and dad.

But then I feel a pull on my arm, and I know that one of the Temple Moor kids has got behind me, and that the end is here. Blindly I spin and lunge, thinking only to scare away the attacker behind me.

But it was not an attacker.

I feel the resistance. The resistance of flesh. Feel the knife first cut, and then meet bone, and then slide off the bone and in, in deep, and I see my hand on the black plastic hilt, and see the white shirt turn red, and then I feel his cheek as he falls against me, and I see his wide staring eye, and in the same instant I know that it is Shane, know not from the sight of him, but from his clean smell, and the aura of goodness.

And at once the others are around us, Billy and Stevie and Maddy and Serena.

"Oh God, what have you done?"

"He was coming to help."

"Someone . . . quick—call an ambulance."

And a bubble of blood forms on his lips and, after a second, pops, the sound as delicate as a raindrop falling on a leaf.

Words, voices, tears, nothing.

TWENTY-NINE

I have visitors. My mother and father come every week. We sit in a bare room, facing each other across a wooden table. On the table there is a vase and in the vase there is a plastic flower. They believe me when I say that I did not mean to hurt Shane. Does that make it easier for them? I think it makes it harder. My father talks about things that are happening in the world. My mother's eyes fill with fat, unfallen tears. I tell them that one day I will come out, and that I will be good.

But how can I be good? Now I have killed a boy, killed him with a knife, how can I ever be good again?

I hoped that Maddy might come to see me, and the other freaks, Billy, Stevie, Serena. I could have explained to them what happened, got them to forgive me. But they will never come, and they will hate me forever. I think about Maddy, and imagine a life we might have had together. Not even a whole life, but just a few months, a year, two years, going out, normal things.

Never, never, never, never, never.

Shane died before he reached the hospital. Hell, he died straightaway. The knife blade bounced off his rib and up into his heart, and his heart stopped, as hearts will. But they tried. Reviving him, I mean. The ambulance guys tried, the ER people tried, the surgeons tried. They took him to the same hospital he'd walked out of an hour earlier.

He'd left Casualty to come and keep me away from the fight. I heard the story in full later, of course. How he'd called the others, told them to help, said that he'd be there soon. That he saw my fight with Mickey, and came to stop me from doing something stupid.

Of course, I wasn't allowed to see him, in the hospital, or afterward. What happened just after I stabbed Shane is a bit murky. You'll probably think that's because I don't want to remember it all, and you're right.

Someone must have told the teachers. The police. The

ambulance. All turned up. The police first. A car pulled up on the road next to the field, and two coppers came running. One fell, and there was laughter—don't know who from. At the first sight of the police, everyone who could run ran. Scattered everywhere. For a while the two policemen tried to grab some of the runners, but it was no use, and anyway they soon realized where the action was. Here, with me and Shane, dying.

People were in my face. Maddy was wailing and crying. I think she hit me. Someone hit me. Perhaps they all hit me. *He was trying to help*, they were shouting. I wanted to tell them about Kirk, how it was all his fault, but nobody listened to me. Before the police reached us, I pushed my way closer to Shane. His eyes were closed, and his body was trembling, just tiny little movements, like a leaf in a breeze. I think I said, *Sorry, sorry, sorry*. And then the trembling stopped.

The police arrested me. They found the knife. Both knives, I mean. The one I'd taken off Mickey, and the one concealed in my pocket. That was the knife that led to my conviction. I'd gone armed to the battle. I was a knife killer.

But I'm alive, so how can I talk about the knife that killed me? Because I'm not alive. Because I died back there on the gypsy field, when I took the life of my friend Shane. Died in my heart, died in my spirit, died in my brain. True, my body moves. Moves from my cell (they call it a room, but it is a cell) to the showers, to the dining hall, to the recreation room, to the toilet, and back to the cell. But what moves is a zombie, an animated corpse. I don't know when I will be set free, but it doesn't matter. Because the chains and the bars are inside me, and I will never be free of them.

I think about Shane all the time. When you kill someone you love, they will be with you forever. I see his face, smiling at me when we first met. See him smiling at other times, down in his basement or in the streets, just hanging out. I hear his quiet voice. I can't quite make out his words, but I know they are wise, and without reproach.

I saw his eyes in his mother's eyes in the court, saw his mouth in his father's mouth.

But Shane is not the only ghost that haunts me. I could live with the ghost of Shane. The ghost of Shane could be my friend. But there is another ghost.

Let me not call him a ghost but a god.

Because Roth is not dead. The rage of the Templars could not kill him. Saved him, in fact. Because he was hurt, the world saw him as a victim. There was no court case for Roth, no charges to answer.

He was in hospital with Shane. But he lived when Shane died. Because, you see, the cruel gods are stronger than the kind gods, and they will always beat them in the end.

You doubt it? Look at the world, my brother, my sister.

And so the spirit of Roth is here with me also, and battles for my soul.

And I don't know who will win.

AUTHOR'S NOTE

The Knife That Killed Me is a story about the excitement, the despair, the joy, and the horror of contemporary teenage life. High school is where things happen: where you find yourself caught up in violence and brutality; where you try to negotiate the labyrinth of power relations; where mistakes can lead to beatings, or worse. But it's also where friendship and love burn like phosphorus in your head.

The setting, the characters, even much of the plot of *The Knife That Killed Me*, came straight out of my own experiences at a tough inner-city school in the industrial north of England. The brutality began with the teachers and passed on down through the school psychos and bullies until it bounced up against the flakes and nerds at the bottom.

And yet for me, those really were the best of times, when anxiety and desire made every day feel special, like a movie, like something that mattered.

The impetus for writing this book was a startling and tragic series of deaths involving teenagers and knives that dominated the news in the UK from 2006 to 2008. It seemed that you couldn't open the newspaper or turn on the TV without staring into the eyes of a kid who'd been stabbed to death, usually by another teenager. It was a new phenomenon in the UK: we suddenly found ourselves in a new place, where the quaintly old-fashioned fist and boot had been replaced by a much more dangerous weapon.

I wanted to write a story that looked beyond the headlines, that strove to see how two young people could find themselves in a situation in which one held the hilt of a knife, and the other folded his guts around the blade.

The Knife That Killed Me is not at all like the other books I've written for young adults. *Hellbent* and *Jack Tumor* are surreal, gross-out comedies, albeit comedies mottled with darkness. *The Knife That Killed Me* is dark all the way through. Instead of making the reader laugh, I want to grip him or her by the throat, gradually increasing the tension until it hurts. It's a harrowing story but, I trust, a compassionate one too.

ABOUT THE AUTHOR

Anthony McGowan was born in Manchester and
brought up in Leeds; he lives in London.
His previous novels for teenagers are
Hellbent and *Jack Tumor*.